FIREFLIES

CHARCO PRESS

First published by Charco Press 2017

Charco Press Ltd., Office 59, 44-46 Morningside Road, Edinburgh EH10 4BF

Work published with funding from the 'Sur' Translation Support Program of
the Ministry of Foreign Affairs and Worship of Argentina / Obra editada en
el marco del Programa 'Sur' de Apoyo a las Traducciones del Ministerio de
Relaciones Exteriores y Culto de la República Argentina.

A CIP catalogue record for this book is available from the British Library.

ISBN: 978 1 9997227 4 6
e-book: 978 1 9997227 5 3

www.charcopress.com

Edited by Annie McDermott
Cover design by Pablo Font
Typeset by Laura Jones

4   6   8   10   9   7   5   3

Luis Sagasti

FIREFLIES

Translated by
Fionn Petch

CHARCO PRESS

CONTENTS

To Camila and Jeremías

There goes Captain Beto through space,
a photo of Carlitos on the console
a pennant of River Plate
and a very sad card of a saint.

LUIS ALBERTO SPINETTA

1. FIREFLIES

The world is a ball of wool.

A skein of yarn you can't find the end of.

When you can't, you pluck at the surface to bring up a strand and then break it with a sharp tug. Once you find the other end, you can tie the two threads of yarn together again. One of grandma's little tricks.

Some people think the world is a ball of wool from a lamb that sacrificed itself long ago so everyone could stay warm.

And they find this idea comforting.

And there are others who think that, in fact, the world is held up by threads. As if the ball of yarn were elsewhere. So headlines appear that try to explain things like *who pulls the strings of the world*. Magazine covers: two threatening eyes against a black background. And there are writers who write whole books about this. Conspiracy theories. An explanation that arises from intellectual laziness: the idea that a shadowy group has chosen to weave the plots of all of our lives. Just like that. Because: a) they are pure and good; b) they want to keep hold of their wealth; c) they are evil, really evil; or d) they hold a secret that would be the end of all of us if we were to find it out – and of them too, of course. For those who see the world this way, any conspiracy – because there have always been conspiracies – is just the visible result of a greater conspiracy. And the smaller conspiracies are all interconnected. Man never reached the moon. Paul McCartney died in 1967 and was replaced by a lookalike. Christ descended from the cross and had twins with Mary Magdalene. Shakespeare's works were actually written by Francis Bacon. The Lautaro Lodge was a branch of the Freemasons, who are a branch of the Rosicrucians, who are a branch of the Gnostics, and the tree proliferates so wildly that not only does it leave us unable to see the wood but it also fills everything with shadows, making way for those two threatening eyes that want us to understand that there's something out there it's better we don't know about. Because – and this we do know – conspirators always leave clues, as if everything were one big game of hide and seek. For people who think like this, any secret is part of the plot because when people conspire they breathe low and in unison, as if whispering a secret.

We shouldn't believe them, though it's right to believe in secrets. After all, childhood is nothing but the progressive revelation of well-kept secrets. To reveal them all at the same time would be to reveal nothing. The darkest dark and the whitest light are equally blinding. Like discovering that your dad has already bought all your Santa presents for the next five years.

How do we know when there are no more secrets? When do we find that out? Or is there nothing to learn?

There are secrets that make the world work in a particular way. But they shouldn't be called secrets. *Omissions* would be more prudent. For the machine to keep running, it's better not to mention certain things. Every family holds a terrible secret that, as soon as we sense what it might be, is no longer mentioned.

And there are still others who believe that these threads in fact sustain the world *from the inside*, as if the world were the great ball of wool and we were insects, like ants or flies, crawling or flying around it. A ball of wool someone is using to knit something. Or perhaps no one is knitting anything at all. There's just a great shroud with no Penelope, growing without purpose in the eternal silence of infinite space.

One thing we can be sure of is that, for hundreds of thousands of years, the ball of yarn has been revolving without pause.

This is something the earliest shamans knew, just by looking at the stars.

In all this, the knitting needles and the resulting scarf or pullover don't look particularly great in the end. Who'd want to try them on? Some god freezing to death in the vastness of space, or some god who *is* space at 270 degrees below zero, immobile, frozen, who observes how every now and again phosphorescent insects – something like fireflies – appear on the revolving ball of yarn, on one side and then the other, as if they could move through it. Traverse it, yes. From side to side. Except these fireflies seem to flee ahead of the needles. Or perhaps they are the needles.

Outside it's cold; up there it's cold. It's true, the stars in the sky burn at hundreds of millions of degrees Celsius, but the voids drawn between them are at absolute zero. The straight line formed by the stars of Orion's belt is an icy needle held at 270 degrees below zero. All the constellations are threaded by icy needles in the image of vast animals hidden somewhere on this planet-like ball of wool.

Among people, we should seek out only the fireflies; the rest are simply animals whose frost is reflected in the heavens.

Should we become fireflies?

Ever since people raised their heads for the first time

to observe the stars and began telling them apart by nothing more than the invisible threads of frozen silver that link them, they also began to tell stories. About why the ball of wool revolves only to return to the same place each year; about who the great weaver is, the great animal, the great reindeer, the great bear, the great hare that knits its pullover with those icy needles in order to warm up those who pass that way once their skin has become as cold as their bones. Those who sleep a dreamless sleep and become, naturally, the dreams of others. Or at least provide source material for their insomnia.

Up there it's so cold. Perhaps that's why the people huddled around the fire tell the story of the great pullover. Time and again. And from up there, sitting on the edges of those icy needles running from star to star, is it possible to see the fire crackling? The light of the caves?

Insect-men, curled up in a ball, gathered around the firefly that illuminates the night with its tale.

It's cold out there. It's always a good idea to start where it's cold, or where there's liquid. That's the point of the ball of wool. To be able to return, later in the story, to the warmth of the good earth.

Where to start, if we can't find the end of the strand and we don't want to break the yarn?

Start with the open mouths of those by the fire listening to the story of the ball of wool, for example. Or the open mouths of those who fall into the cold.

The mouth opens whenever it's the *first time*. It imitates the frozen abyss that separates the stars.

In the beginning and in the end the breath stops. Always. The mouth opens wider. Or the eyes, those two mouths that swallow everything. The world fits into the body and once it occupies it completely, it explodes against the ground or emerges in a shout. Or a sigh.

One, two, three and the *four* that's left unspoken, the band holds its breath, and there, the music of the spheres begins to play.

2. HAIKUS

In the winter of 1943, one of the cruellest in living memory, perhaps because no one had anything in their bellies, the Stuka being flown by the officer Joseph Beuys was hit by a Russian fighter plane after a brief combat in the skies above Crimea. Beneath them, the cold was turning the pine needles into crystals, transforming the trees into a translucent forest of blue mirrors that smash the aircraft into hundreds of pieces before it even reaches the ground. Beuys' face, already shattered, streaks past the tiny mirrors of ice hanging from the branches. Mirrors of ice like perfect, diminutive haikus. Everything takes just a few hundred years that somehow fit into the blink of an eye. It has been snowing steadily for almost two days, scattering particles of silence over the branches and across the ground. The snow absorbs part of the noise of the plummeting aircraft, but the sound of thousands of breaking mirrors reaches the alert ears of the Tatars. The pilot's skill or luck meant the plane didn't land on its nose and explode. Officer Beuys, gravely wounded, unconscious and near-frozen, is rescued by a group of nomad Tatars who know nothing about the war. They've come to understand that when there's thunder above but no storm, it's best to take refuge beneath the biggest trees. The co-pilot has broken his neck. His name was Karl Vogts. His body is never found.

For a period of time Beuys cannot calculate, he is

stalked by death, which is only kept at bay by the Tatar shaman who smears the pilot's wounds with animal fat and wraps him in felt. Hare skins are the best choice when it comes to protecting someone from the cold. He recites the prayers he's learnt on one of the three nights when the moon disappears. Days pass, and death leaves to maraud elsewhere. When he regains consciousness, the aviator starts to speak in an unintelligible language made up of words born of fever, inseparable one from the other, even for the shaman, who knows the tongue of the animals. The man who fell from the plane has blue eyes and full lips. He is too dazed for fear to express itself in his face. The Tatars keep him awake for most of the day, always wrapped tightly in the felt blanket, like a mummy. He lies trembling before a hearth where the fire is never allowed to go out. He is not sure when he is dreaming and when he is awake, if it is cold or if it is warm. He thinks he wakes up in the middle of the night. He sees things. Or perhaps he sees nothing. It is more likely he sees nothing. His mind is a burning pot. Neurons like thousands of still mirrors reflecting without judging – this is their fidelity. The Tatars pass in front of him, blurs of light. The faces come from above, as if falling before his eyes. Some smile, others look at him in amazement. The shaman appears when night falls and Beuys sees that his head is on fire. Years later, he would recall being inside a large tent. The roof was faded blue and he could make out a series of – painted? embroidered? – yellow and white stars.

'I tried to identify a constellation but I couldn't: the stars shifted every time I looked at them.'

Once, the shaman points to an empty space between the stars and says something Beuys is unable to pronounce. But this word, which the shaman repeats again and again, pointing to the empty space between the stars, calms him.

What they give Beuys to eat is also a mystery, but the strength gradually returns to his body. One day he gets up, leaves the tent and is able to walk a few steps unassisted. The Tatars follow him with their eyes. A little boy hides behind his mother, peeking out at the pilot. Beuys turns around, and the shaman smiles back at him.

Two or three days after this, he is rescued by a German patrol. Beuys completes his convalescence in a field hospital. The man who a month later returns to the front is a changed person, who will be successively decorated for bravery, demoted for rebelliousness, captured by the British and finally repatriated to Germany once the war is over. The scars on his head will be covered by a felt trilby hat. Long leather coats, and sometimes fisherman's vests, complete his outfit. Very few pictures show him without this uniform. Twenty-five years after the events in Crimea, Joseph Beuys had become one of the most influential artists in the world.

In 1969, Kurt Vonnegut published *Slaughterhouse-Five*. The flagship of my little fleet, he declares in a news item. However we read it, and there are many ways of doing so, it will always be counted among the top five candidates for the Great American Novel of the twentieth century. In 1944, Vonnegut was taken prisoner by the Germans following the Battle of the Bulge. He was transferred and locked up in slaughterhouse number five in the city of Dresden.

The beauty of this city was a magnet that attracted the Allies' wrath, and the Florence on the Elbe, as it was known, was destroyed by bombs in February 1945. The Germans had shown no mercy with Coventry a few years earlier, and now they would learn their lesson: never touch the crown jewels. Vonnegut was one of seven Americans to survive. One week before the bombing, his mother committed suicide in Chicago. Vonnegut would make his own attempt, without success, in 1985. The cocktail of pills and alcohol he prepared was the same as that his mother had taken. After the war, Vonnegut settled in New York. More than a cynic, the war had turned him into a chronic depressive, who drank and smoked to excess.

The protagonist of *Slaughterhouse-Five* is called Billy Pilgrim, and it's self-evident that he's an alter ego of Vonnegut. Billy can travel to different moments, both past and future, of his own life. It happens to him involuntarily. In the novel's first pages, Vonnegut writes that many years after the war, the aeroplane carrying Billy Pilgrim from Ilium to Montreal crashed into the peak of Sugarbush Mountain in Vermont. All those on board died except Bill. The accident 'left him with a terrible scar on the top of his skull'.

After this accident, Billy Pilgrim began to say that he had been kidnapped by aliens from the planet Tralfamadore.

In October 1992, the state museum of Gelsenkirchen published a selection of work by Joseph Beuys entitled *Mensch, Natur und Kosmos*. The volume includes a short introductory study by the art historian Franz van der Grinten, and consists of a series of watercolours painted by Beuys between 1948 and 1957, sketched on file cards or in notebooks. The largest measures thirty-two by twenty centimetres and, even though it's a high-quality publication, the pencil outline of most of them is so faint that the forms are hard to distinguish. Crows, women, water and trees, painted as if with moonlight. In the earliest drawings, however, the lines and the colours are more dynamic. On the cover there is a particularly energetic drawing: a crow, the first in an unseen series, two women, perhaps, and in the background an erupting volcano or a tree, who knows, all sketched out with abrupt, blue, nervous lines.

There is a sometimes astonishing similarity between the watercolours painted by Beuys after the war, around 1955, and the sketches for *The Little Prince* by Antoine de Saint-Exupéry. A yellowish-amber hue predominates in both, and the figures are weightless and unsupported. The bodies are barely defined by patches of colour. In the case of Saint-Exupéry, who was not a painter, it is obvious that they are sketches, a first attempt at something that is far from definitive. In contrast, Beuys, who by now has returned from the war, knows he can do nothing but sketch, nothing but promise what will never be realised; his watercolours are an image of what is to come (and what it is hoped never does come). One of Saint-Exupéry's drawings is of a sleeping fox; the marks delineate the restless outline, over and over, the line itself vacillating; or rather, the fox is not sleeping, though it gives the impression of doing so; or, to put it better, no fox could ever sleep with such an agitated, hesitant body. Beneath it on the same page is something that looks like a puma. It is upside down, as if it were buried underground and digging itself out to meet the body of the fox.

Beuys prefers to draw other animals. Elks, for example. Beneath the deer on the front cover of his *Early Watercolours*, there is a sun, its rays piercing the animal. Many of Beuys' drawings are barely decipherable, just charcoal on tracing paper. Even so, his confident hand is always in evidence. For the German artist, an animal is a kind of angelic being. This idea comes not only from his reading of Rudolf Steiner, founder of the philosophical current known as anthroposophy, but also from his time

11

with the Tatar nomads. Indeed, while he was delirious with fever in the forests of Crimea, wrapped in felt and smeared in fat, an elk appeared to him. A giant one, like the megatherium species. A megatherian elk or megaelk that starts to dance before his eyes. Beuys hears the Tatar tambourines and flutes made with the bones of these very elks. He said later that as soon as the melody ended, the elk transformed into a shaman. He shivers because he's hot and he's cold. The Tatars begin to pack up the camp swiftly and silently. It seems someone has warned them the Russians are approaching. They damp down the fires. From above, a stampede of fireflies appears. The Tatars flee towards the west, which is where Beuys' plane came down. They put him on a horse, laying him crosswise over the horse's back and tying him down. Beuys presses his stomach against the animal's flank, and when it begins to trot he abruptly vomits.

'I vomited up the stars from the shaman's tent. Yellow and white stars.'

Everything is thick and shiny.

Billy Pilgrim will return to Dresden, to the slaughter-house five where his life was saved, on several occasions. On one of his journeys through time he has the bad luck to be abducted by an alien civilisation that takes him to the planet Tralfamadore, where he is exhibited in a kind of intergalactic zoo together with a woman named Montana Wildhack. Vonnegut tells us nothing about how they got there, nor about how they freed themselves. Pilgrim's daughter thinks the war has driven her father crazy.

Slaughterhouse-Five can be read in many different ways. The three leading candidates are: as the hallucinations of a soldier injured in the war, as the ramblings of an old veteran, and perhaps as an extraordinary tale of autobiographical science fiction – if such a thing could exist outside of the work of Philip K. Dick. However it is approached, though, the most interesting pages of the book are those dedicated to explaining the literature of Tralfamadore. 'Brief clumps of symbols separated by stars [...] each clump of symbols is a brief, urgent message, describing a situation, a scene. We Tralfamadorians read them all at once, not one after the other.' Without causes or effects: 'what we love in our books are the depths of many marvellous moments seen all at one time'.

In some sense Joseph Beuys never left the forests of Crimea, and some of his most celebrated performances bear witness to this fact. In May 1974, in the Block Gallery in New York, he performed *I Like America and America Likes Me*. In protest against the Vietnam War, Beuys decided to avoid setting foot on U.S. soil as far as possible. He arrived at John F. Kennedy airport, was put straight into an ambulance and then taken directly to the room containing a coyote, where he remained for three days. Beuys covered himself with a felt cape. He carried a stick and never took off his hat.

A few years earlier he presented his most famous performance: *How to Explain Pictures to a Dead Hare*. This is the first time Beuys appears in public without a hat. With his head covered with honey and sprinkled with gold dust, he holds up a dead hare and tries to explain the meaning of art to it. His head is illuminated, as if a soft, sweet light were emanating from his war wounds.

Light is coming out of Beuys' head.

Like the horns of Michelangelo's Moses: a marble light that transforms him into the Devil, into Lucifer.

Shamans travel into the skies in search of the sick person's soul in order to return it to their body.

Where did the hare's soul go? Is there a heaven for hares? When you're little you imagine there must be a heaven for animals. Never a hell. Your pet dog doesn't go to hell. Though the only thing we are sure of is that hell is full of monstrous, repugnant animals. Not heaven, though; there are no animals in heaven. Except for in clan cultures: the great bear, the great reindeer.

Fly up to the heaven of the golden hares.

Sometimes, the return to Crimea is more traumatic: Beuys suffers from severe convulsions, exhausting spasms, which he ends up turning into performances. One of these becomes the December 1966 work *Manresa*, in which Beuys presents one half of a cross wrapped in felt and the other drawn on a blackboard. Felt and fat are placed at each corner. As he paces about the room, Beuys asks after the third element; that is, the precise midpoint between intuition and reason.

Months earlier, he had visited the Spanish city of Manresa, where in 1522 Saint Ignatius wrote his *Spiritual Exercises*. There, Beuys suffered a sudden attack, a kind of nervous breakdown. Draped over the back of the horse trotting through the wood, he has nothing left to vomit. It's not only his stomach that feels empty but his whole body, as if he had no organs. Dozens of hares accompany him. The scene resembles a panel from the comic strip *Little Nemo in Slumberland*. The procession is led by a hare that is sometimes an elk and that never loses its light. Beuys' head is swathed in felt. It is throbbing. And the pain is like boiling water running down the furrows of his scars. Behind him he hears voices closing in on him. There is no snow on the trees. Everything is mud and noise.

He wakes up in the hospital in Manresa. Beside him is

Per Kirkeby, the artist he had come on holiday with. Beuys looks at him and smiles, unconcerned. The ceiling of the room is pale cream in colour. He wants to leave.

The haiku is the closest we have come to writing the way they do in Tralfamadore. Expressing in an instant what happens over time. The motionless stone that shimmers in the light: this stone both is and is not this stone and so it will go on, regardless of the fact that 2500 years ago the Greeks began to argue about the nature of things and the discussion has never let up since.

How many words can be read at once without shifting the gaze? Two, three, maybe four. It has to be a prime number. Five is too many. Three, then, is a safe bet. Any more and the gaze clouds over, the words escape around the edges and form a virtual, magnetic zone of attraction that pulls the eyes to one side or the other. The gaze cannot rest on the present moment of the sentence because it seeks symmetry. Four words are two plus two, for example. The sequential character of language is an impassable barrier in our alphabetic systems. Only a haiku written in Japanese can halt the train of language and cast an anchor into the present, the motionless stone lit up by the sun in the morning and the evening. And as we follow the words with the gaze, how many words is it possible to read without punctuation marks? How far can we carry on before we lose the meaning or get lost in the meanders and have to go back? There, in the middle of the river, who is responsible for ensuring the ship does not get trapped in the weeds? The writer? The reader?

How many words without shifting the gaze? Perhaps pairs of words that have been fused by their sound. *What's up?* for example.

A Japanese haiku comprises seventeen moras, which are something like the atoms of language. Phonemes are smaller still and have no real body to them, like electrons and other theoretical particles that vibrate nervously in the imagination. Pure formal abstraction.

Are these seventeen moras the measure of the present moment?

Etymology bursts with meanings. The word *mora* comes from the Latin for 'linger, delay' and was used to translate the Greek word *chronos* in its metrical sense.

The seventeen moras are divided into three verses of five, seven and five. An expert calligrapher can lay down the Japanese characters in such a way that they are taken in almost at a single glance. Language and perception conjoined. So it is impossible to translate a haiku, to write a haiku. Our language dilates, delays, demurs what should be a clean *tock!* on the Zen wood. These three words that can be perceived at a glance: that is as far as the impossible translation of a haiku can go. Conventionally, versions of haikus in Western languages use three verses of five, seven and five syllables each. But this is a pretty poor and distant imitation of their true attributes, even though curiously enough they tend to be shorter when read out loud.

In 1682, after spending two days shut up in the cabin his disciples had built for him on the other side of a raging river so he could cultivate his poetry in solitude, Matsuo Basho, the most celebrated author of haikus in Japan, which is to say the world, set it on fire. The only thing he had with him when two disciples helped him to cross back over the river was a sheet of paper on which he appeared to have written a haiku. No one verified the story. The fire was accidental. Around this time, Basho had received the news that his mother was dead. And it was believed that these two strokes of misfortune were somehow connected. But one of the twenty disciples let slip many years later, when Basho was more interested in frogs jumping into pools, that he had seen someone leave the cabin as evening fell, the day before the fire. And it was not just anyone.

Matsuo Basho was born the son of a samurai in 1644 and lived for fifty years. The closest he came to his father's destiny was joining the service of another samurai, with whom he would later write poems. His real name was Matsuo Kinsaku. He adopted the name Basho when his disciples planted a banana tree (*basho* in Japanese) beside his cabin. After the fire, Basho embarked on the first of his four journeys through Japan. He abandoned his disciples and all vestiges of social life and began an austere pilgrimage that steadily whittled away at his poems until they reached the most complex of simplicities. His final work is entitled *Oku no Hosomichi* (*The Narrow Road to the Deep North*) and is a kind of diary of the fourth journey he undertook, with a disciple named Sora. Over five months they travelled more than 1,200 miles, visiting the furthest reaches of northern Japan. A pilgrimage where Santiago de Compostela could be found in the most unsuspecting cherry tree.

At that time it was widely believed (and many scholars still believe it today) that Kioyi Hatasuko, a contemporary of Basho, was the greatest calligrapher of haikus. His lines were produced in a single motion, wrist and forearm moving to and fro like those of an orchestra conductor. Involuntary lashes of a whip; Jackson Pollock chasing a fly with his paintbrush. When Kioyi Hatasuko wrote his own haikus, he would spend almost the whole afternoon sitting facing a landscape. Then, with two or three gestures, he laid down the ink on the paper. What is curious is that his own haikus were not considered good enough. The meaning of the poems could be captured immediately, and in this sense his technique was astonishing, but the content, the poetic vision if we can call it that, was lacking. Hatasuko knew the value of his haikus; there was truth in the spontaneity of his lines, but sometimes truth can be a bit insipid. He never achieved the simplicity of Basho. His best-known haiku reads:

Between the lightning and the thunder
A bird
Seeks refuge

Basho took a different approach, in which perception and creation were almost irreconcilable. The sure hand evident in his calligraphy was the fruit of strenuous effort, and this wasn't easy to disguise.

If we ignore what the disciple claims to have seen the day before the fire, Basho and Hatasuko – who were nearly the same age – never actually met. But there is another version of the story. It is said that one day Hatasuko was so moved by one of Basho's haikus that he decided to visit him, though he knew the poet rarely received anyone in his cabin. As for Basho, he admired Hatasuko's calligraphy but knew that his haikus were less than brilliant.

The poets met one morning beneath the banana tree. Autumn was in the air. Basho had been contemplating the river since the morning, wearing a simple tunic. They went inside the cabin. The host served tea. At some point, Hatasuko asked Basho for a blank sheet of paper, a brush and some ink.

'I want you to show me your haikus. It is my wish to

write my own haiku based on the impressions they evoke,' he said.

Basho brought him ink, paper and brush and began to show him his work. The visitor limited himself to smiling, occasionally making an exclamation or chuckling. His right wrist rested on the edge of the table, the brush held between thumb and forefinger. His hand was in a state of tense repose. Without making a gesture or saying a word, Basho laid down sheet after sheet. There was no regularity in his movements. Sometimes he would produce two or three sheets at once; sometimes he would sit for half an hour in silence with his gaze resting on some object in the room. Every once in a while he poured tea for them both. The sun was sinking low in the sky by the time Basho showed Hatasuko his final haiku. Like a cornered panther, Hatasuko traced the characters in the blink of an eye. A pool that reflects the image all at once. Then he remained still for a while, gazing at the sheet without saying a word. When the ink had dried, he turned it around and showed it to Basho. The strokes were perfect, a black river that began in a pool and here broadened out, there narrowed to nothing, before re-emerging in a slender line that bifurcated and turned back on itself in a broad flourish. The characters (if indeed that is what they were) could barely be distinguished. After a while Hatasuko got up to leave, and they bid each other farewell in silence.

Basho kept the painting.

And it would seem that he meant to set fire to the tree, not his cabin.

During his final journey through the north of Japan, he received the news that Hatasuko had been killed in a fight between two feudal families.

His disciple Sora wrote:

19

My gaze alights on the cherry tree
In the heat of the battle
Now immortal

Coca-Cola! is a perfect haiku: at a single glance colours and flavours follow the shape of the words. Is the exclamation mark at the end really necessary? Because Coca-Cola is already children shouting, bubbles rising to the rim of the glass, the plastic taste of the disposable cups at birthday parties. *Enjoy Coca-Cola, Coke is it, Always Coca-Cola, Coke adds life.* A third word always seems to go well with *Coca-Cola.* And a well-designed slogan should have the power of a haiku. Though *Coca-Cola* doesn't even need the slogan. If the hard *c* didn't create such a staccato effect, it could even be a mantra.

Three words where all you need is the first and last letter in order to understand them: the order of the other letters can be deduced from the context, no special skill required. Texts demonstrating this do the rounds on the Internet, and it is always astonishing how easy they are to read.

The perfect haiku is therefore a single mistyped word in a sentence. One letter out of place, a sudden dyslexia that leaves the mouth open and the eyes staring, stunned by a phoneme never before pronounced. A crack opens up in perception, and immediately closes again. If, as many would have it, words are a reflection of the world, crawling through such cracks means embarking, like Alice, on an adventure into a world that was right under our noses the whole time. That is why the supreme art of many writers lies in discovering the reverse side of the word even while writing it correctly, as if leaving the door ajar. Perhaps this can be done by placing exactly the right word beside it. As if one were the lock, and the other the key.

But these kinds of dyslexic mistakes are no simple printing error, and if they are well done then the rabbit will escape even the most eagle-eyed proofreader. What is odd is that whoever notices such a crack in a word can never convey the sense of discovery to anyone else, but nor can they keep the secret to themselves.

Computer software automatically corrects mistyped words. The words have locks. Cyberspace is smooth and uniform. There are no cracks in the surface: we only find what we are looking for.

When a child learns to read they advance cautiously, letter by letter, then syllable by syllable, committing a route to memory to make sure they never get lost, in the fear of falling back into the well they have emerged from. Learning to read means ascending a staircase that leads only to a level plain.

And this is all there is.

A small roof terrace where the stars of space have lost their virginity and can only be seen because the theory of staircases makes it possible. It is impossible to descend from this terrace and it is impossible to go any further. The paving slabs are variegated. The only way of escaping the terrace is, of course, haiku, the literature of Tralfamadore. The frog leaping in the pool, the loose slab with water beneath.

They say that in the middle of a battle the combination of adrenaline and exhaustion means that suddenly, out of the corner of the eye, black holes can be seen for an instant. (Something similar occurs in extreme cold. Each vertebra of the backbone becomes a snowy peak. A space opens up in the spine like the ones dyslexia opens in words. The spinal cord exposed.)

Going back to Beuys' book and wondering whether we should see conceptual art as a possible way of translating the haiku. An installation that awaits dyslexia, a kind of perceptive discontinuity.

Haikus replace the sense of sight with that of taste. Reading them is like eating a lozenge. There is no history in the taste of honey. The taste of honey is homogenous, at once impetuous and slow. It is the opposite of those wines described as *full-bodied*, which linger on the tongue, wines in which different flavours dwell that can be awoken with a gentle swirling of the glass, lazily unfurling first the red berries, then the cinnamon, followed by the leather, and finally the roast chicken. Wines tell stories. They are not haiku flavours. Or the other way around. If the wine achieves a haiku flavour, its simplicity is reflected in its cost. Wine invokes memory, and it had better have some story to tell in order to stir our own. A honey lozenge is tasted and that's it. It languishes on the tongue. It flows over the taste buds and slowly fades.

Is it not true that in the lines on the face of someone who has really lived – who has battled furiously against the waves and refused to drift through the years as if we had thousands to play with – we can read their entire biography? A whole life at a glance.

It is first in Beuys' skull and then in his face that his biography becomes a haiku. A biography that he covers up as best he can with his felt trilby hats, because what matters is the art emerging from the crevasses in his head. Or if he does take off his hat, he covers his head with honey and gold dust and the years fall away, back to zero, because like this, his face covered, he becomes the shaman carrying out his most famous performance; explaining art to a dead hare. We understand it without even hearing the words.

Before the war, Dresden was home to the largest zoo in Europe. There is no need to list all the animals it contained. The ones you find in any zoo, plus polar bears, crocodiles, a huge serpentarium. When Billy Pilgrim emerged from slaughterhouse five after the bombing, he says, he had actually landed on the moon. There was nothing but craters. The reality was worse, of course. Because as well as everything else, hungry animals were on the loose. And animals falling from the sky in flames. In a war, the first to eat are the ones who negotiate, followed by those who give orders, then those who fight, and then, if there is anything left, the civilians – women and children first – but the animals don't come into the picture. In fact, in the final months the smaller animals in Dresden Zoo were fed to the larger ones. Dogs and cats were no longer to be found even on the plates of colonels. Deer and hares, not a trace. Capybaras, zebras, two gazelles. Each night the keeper took an animal – a capybara, a zebra, a gazelle – and left it in the lion's cage, or in the bear's. The keeper as guardian of the last surviving species. Theory must be implemented in practice even though everything is in flames. Survival of the fittest. But after the 13th of February, when Dresden became the moon, the animals escaped. It was another planet. It was the zoo of Tralfamadore, with the cage doors swinging open. After the bombs had fallen, survivors had to flee not only exploding gas cylinders but the animals too. The most dangerous ones were not the lions or bears – though they did eat a couple of Germans before slowly, clumsily fleeing the bombs and fires – but the crocodiles, which couldn't be seen, but were stumbled across like tree trunks in the mud.

The worst thing I saw in the war, answers Bob Barrel, from Clayton, North Carolina, in the documentary *Dresden Seven*, dedicated to the seven survivors of the massacre, was two lions eating a German family. They survive the bombing only to be eaten by lions. Barrel can't go on and begins to weep.

Vonnegut: I saw giraffes. And yes, I heard about lions eating people. A soldier, Barrel or something, came back terrified one day, shouting about lions. But they would have shot them right away. They said the real danger was the crocodiles. It's like a joke. How to distinguish a crocodile among the rubble? Who's expecting to find one there, right? Eaten by a crocodile in Germany in winter. Christ.

Craig Ehlo, from Lincoln, Nebraska: people talked about lions. I think I saw giraffes in flames, and in a painting too. They were blue. Whatever, we were screwed up at the time. Maybe we still are.

At the opening of his show *Drawings 1946-1971* at the Haus Lange Museum in Krefeld, Beuys was approached by a severe, wiry woman of over 70. She had come from Dusseldorf. Ute introduces herself. Ute Vogts. Beuys smiles despite the woman's dour face. It is unusual to see older people at an opening unless they have come to complain about the state of modern art or the waste of public money on things no one understands however often they have it explained to them. But this woman declares she has come from Dusseldorf especially. Beuys finds this strange because, after all, this is no great feat: Dusseldorf is only a few miles away. But the woman is old and perhaps it was a great effort for her. Perhaps she was drawn there by curiosity. Though by now the Fluxus group has already dissolved and, while Beuys is a celebrity, his exhibitions are no longer the talk of the town. It seems that Ute Vogts is not interested in the art. Her gaze is gentle, despite her piercing blue eyes. Beuys' smile is contagious. The woman smiles back and, as if it were a reaction, begins to blink continuously.

'Where is Karl?' she asks.

'Karl?'

She explains that she is the mother of Karl Vogts, the pilot who was with Beuys in the aeroplane that crashed in Crimea. Beuys falls silent.

'Where is Karl?'

Beuys' deep blue eyes seem to have cracked. He places his hands on the woman's shoulders. She blinks awkwardly. And she asks him: 'Is the story of the Tatars true? Is Karl with the Tatars?'

Beuys removes his felt hat and holds it to his chest. The woman gazes at the scars and understand what she needs to understand.

The hare understands art.

Is there anything to understand?

Without the slightest doubt, art is the answer.

What we can't be sure about is the question.

The moon has descended over Dresden (and will remain there for several years). Vonnegut is ordered to line up the bodies of the dead. Islands of fire in a sea of rubble, smoking flesh, birds falling in flames from the sky. Fireflies are what they resemble. Nearly three days without sleep. Dreaming on his feet. When he returns to the slaughterhouse, where he is still accommodated (if that is the right word), a pile of bodies catches his eye. He thinks he recognises his mother.

He wants to turn back but the Germans force him to continue walking.

Gustav Krauss was one of the soldiers who rescued Beuys.

'We found him inside the plane. His companion was dead,' he tells a local journalist when a controversy arises about the artist's work.

In the end the news goes unremarked, and isn't taken up by the cultural supplements. Germany was playing against England in the final of the World Cup at the time. Just one journalist, Sepp Schwartzmann, takes an interest in the matter. He carries out a less-than-exhaustive investigation. No archives or war logs survived the advance of the Russian front, obviously. There are conjectures. A crack. But Krauss is adamant. They found Beuys unconscious in the cabin of the aircraft. They didn't see anyone else.

There are no nomadic Tatars.

Deeply affronted, Beuys refuses to say another word on the matter.

After the war, the Tatars — nomadic or otherwise — were unfairly accused of collaboration with the Nazis. Other peoples, including the Karachays, the Kalmuks and the Ingush, suffered the same fate. When Stalin's troops recovered Crimea, which had been taken by the Nazis in 1941, the Tatars were deported. This happened on the 17th of May, 1944. One hundred and ninety thousand people were exiled to Central Russia, Uzbekistan, Kazakhstan. The same as the number of Germans who died in Dresden. Mosques and all other buildings relating to their culture were destroyed. The nomads were detained and packed like animals onto trains, just as the Germans had transported the Jews to the *Lager*. Around one third died on the journey. The young and the old, whose thread of life is thinner, die first. They die singing a single-chord song, barely a whisper, that tells of the country where the hares provide shelter for what remains of eternity.

A Soviet patrol came across Beuys' Tatars taking refuge on a thickly-forested hillside. The shaman who knows how to talk to animals doesn't know how to talk to the Russians. Two shots, one in the forehead and the other to scare the rest.

A young man named Tomek travels in one of the wagons where more survived than in others. He had helped get the two German airmen out of the crashed Stuka. He had also hunted the hares to produce the felt they used to wrap the man with the deep blue eyes who had received the terrible wounds to his head. Now it is he, Tomek, whose head is bruised and who is suffering from the cold that enters between the wooden slats – though at least air is getting in – while a dead Tatar rests against his shoulders, his mouth open, dried spittle on his chin. Tomek continues the song his companion had begun, to make sure he reaches the land of the burning hares.

Was Beuys' mouth wide open as his plane fell from the sky? Did his life flash before his eyes as it is said to do, when all the accumulated days rise up from the stomach and force the mouth wide open one last time? Do they rise? Or is it that an abyss opens in the body so the days can enter in an instant? But you have not died, Beuys, or perhaps yes, you have died. Before, you were something else. The mouth that opens is a cervical passage and the final scream is the same scream as that emitted by the mother at the moment the child is born. A scream is always for the first time. Like honey, the scream has no history. It may come before or after something else, but above all it is a pause. A scream always happens for the first time. And everyone always screams at the same frequency. It is impossible to scream out of tune because the succession of notes is interrupted. The scream is a zero, an egg, pure immaculate whiteness. The scream as light. Don't people talk louder at night? Don't they scream better at night, when all things are resolved into one? It is the scream that liberates us from History, from our own personal history. That was what John Lennon screamed in 'Mother' to free himself from so much abandonment.

The hatless head of Beuys, the scars, are truly terrifying.

At the same moment in 1943 that these wounds were formed, wounds that were to go on to synthesise past and future, someone who much later would become one of the world's most important philosophers was writing an enthusiastic letter to a friend, one Hans-Ulrich Wehler, on a sheet of paper bearing a Hitler Youth letterhead. The philosopher is Jürgen Habermas. But at this moment he is twelve years old and his impulsive action demands an apology that will never be forthcoming, according to the account of Joachim Fest, former culture editor of the *Frankfurter Allgemeine Zeitung*, in his memoir *Ich Nicht*. A long time later, the story goes, Wehler invited Habermas for a coffee. They had not seen each other for six or seven years. 'I have a surprise for you,' he tells him by telephone, in a neutral voice. Intrigued, Habermas agrees to meet the next day, mid-morning. His impatience exaggerates his German punctuality: Habermas arrives ten minutes early and asks for a coffee. Wehler arrives at the agreed hour, not a minute later. The philosopher has already finished his first espresso. His friend asks for the same, a double. Initially, they make small talk. As if he suspects something, Habermas reduces the intervening years to broad brushstrokes: a couple of books published, teaching, his marriage, a flood. Wehler takes his time, and once the waiter has brought him his coffee he begins rooting around in his jacket pockets. Look what I found, he says with a half-smile, and hands over a faded yellow envelope. Habermas thinks he knows what is inside. He opens it slowly, as if it were a letter bomb. He needs only a glance to recognise the prolix, insistent lines, with emphasis placed on certain words. Wehler concentrates on stirring his coffee. Habermas neither knows nor cares what is behind that smile, it is enough to know what stands in front of this letter. A procession 2,500 years long, led by Thales and with Heidegger bringing up the rear, flashes by, and as it does so it opens his mouth wider and wider onto the abyss of non-being. Habermas folds the letter into a wad, puts it in his mouth and begins to chew. Wehler watches, astonished, frozen in the motion of stirring his coffee. The philosopher can't get all of the paper down, grabs his friend's cup and empties it in one gulp. It is boiling hot. He turns red and all but shouts at the waiter for a glass of water. Eventually, Wehler bursts out laughing. To break the spell.

The torn leaves fall trembling into Habermas's stomach. A digestive autumn. The words are stuck together with saliva and form new words that pass through the black hole of the larynx to the inner abysses, words whose readers are the inhabitants of the planet Trafalmadore, and later Billy Pilgrim, outside the book, once he learns this language. Down they fall, these gobbets of paper that only exist in the present moment. Strangers to philosophy and close to Zen, close to Heidegger in the forests of Freiburg when he realised that truth cannot be reached with words. (Words can construct truth but never reach it.) Everything is the present,

Habermas: the Führer's troops parading, your parents' pride at seeing you there on the street, looking so smart.

And how is everything going back on the outside? The philosopher has returned to his normal colour. He runs his tongue across his teeth. With his tongue, he writes a final story in Tralfamadorian. A flavour with no history. A flavourless boiled sweet from his childhood, when sweets ran out in Germany in 1944.

'I have a photocopy for dessert,' his friend says. He's jesting. Or is he?

'Don't even joke about it,' Habermas says.

When he was little, Saint-Exupéry drew a picture of a boa constrictor that had eaten an elephant, and no one was frightened because all they saw was a hat. Why be scared of a hat? Which head does it fit?

The reverse of Tralfamadore is found on the back cover of the paperback Spanish translation published by Anagrama, which gives it as *Trafalmadore*.

Tomek has seen many things in the war. Crevasses, haikus, spinal columns rising up from the ground as if the Russian plains were the back of a writhing monster. Tomek has survived the journey to Siberia. The cold, the grey air. After the war he ends up in Novosibirsk, working in a steel foundry. He has married a Tatar woman. Their children speak Tatar and Russian. Tatar at home. The parents are learning Russian, while the children talk at school as if they're walking across rice paper: not a single word in Tatar, not a single word incorrectly written or spoken in Russian.

Or else: dyslexia, haikus and the teacher's open mouth; from there the party commissar is just a step away, and a sentence using the wrong case will get you sent there in a flash. *The Little Prince* was translated into Russian in 1950. Every child reads the book. The translation into Tatar only appeared in 2000. Latinised, the title is *Näni Prins*. It is the only edition on the planet that doesn't show a drawing by Saint-Exupéry on the cover. Though the lines are similar, there is something soft about it that doesn't reflect his hand. It looks like a sketch. You can see it clearly on the Internet. Tomek buys the book for his grandchildren. The book gives no indication of who did the cover drawing. It doesn't matter to Tomek. He plods clumsily through the snow of Novosibirsk. We know he has been a widower for some time, and has lost one of his three children. He lives alone, a few streets from his daughter, who was the middle child and is now the youngest. Tomek kicks the snow from his boots before entering her house. His daughter kisses him on the cheek; her husband is in the kitchen cooking fish. The children are watching television; the youngest runs into his arms.

After dinner, Tomek presents his grandchildren with their gift. They squint to read the title in Tatar. Their grandfather sits in an armchair – his armchair – and begins to read to them. After five minutes, the children are bored. Why don't you tell us, the oldest asks him, the story of the pilot who crashed in the forest?

It's important to think carefully about the first story you tell a child or grandchild, because it's the one you'll be condemned to repeat. Just as a hit single will come to be an albatross for a rock band.

The thunderbolt-skipping pilot had come down in the middle of the forest and his aircraft was smashed to pieces, never to fly again. That's how the story always starts. After that, Grandpa Tomek is corrected every time he strays off course or, over time, adds insignificant or horrific details, like when he describes the pilot's head furrowed with scars that looked like lightning bolts. Even though he is not fully recovered, the shaman's medicines have made him feel a lot better. One stormy night he feels his spirits returning and decides to help two men search for firewood before the rains arrive. They walk through the forest until the path leads them to the edge of a frozen lake. It is a large lake and the storm is reflected on the blue-white surface. It's like seeing the sky upside-down. Suddenly the pilot begins to run from spot to spot, stamping on the lightning bolts as they flash on the ice. The two Tatars who are with him drop the branches they are carrying and also begin to run. The pilot, wrapped in his felt cape, laughs wildly and counts the lighting bolts he steps on.

And since the thunderclaps are getting louder and louder, but the rain is still holding off, the pilot feels like he is dancing above the sky. He thinks he'll never get wet. And seemingly he begins to sing, together with the Tatars. A child like Tomek has no problem understanding his strange language.

When he reaches the part about the dance, the grandfather pauses, as they have all been expecting him to. At this point he always says: and in one of his leaps the pilot comes down where the ice is thinner. The ice cracks as if it were his own face, a hole opens up and he falls into the water. The younger grandchild always bursts out laughing here, just like his mother did when she was little. They get him out soaking wet and have to warm him up by the fire. But Grandfather Tomek knows this isn't true, that the pilot didn't fall into the water but carried on treading on the lightning and dancing until he was knocked down by an exhaustion that was like a shard of fever. They dragged themselves back to the camp. And that night, despite all the lightning, it didn't rain.

And Beuys' hats were as famous as his art. Like Glenn Gould's chair, or John Lennon's glasses.

Ungaretti. We should tip our hats on hearing the name of someone who refused to shed a single tear for himself in any of the letters he sent from the battlefront. The recipient of these letters was his friend and first publisher, Gherardo Marone. Without complaint or lament, in each missive Giuseppe Ungaretti displays a veritable *ars poetica* with the power of a howitzer, and the letters sometimes say things to which the only response can be silence. Such as: *Let us not resist life. And the purest poetry will emerge.* As Italy earns itself new and different enemies, Ungaretti, who has signed up as a volunteer, will fight in France and, later, in the Carso region near Trieste.

Adjectives conceal the true *presence* of objects: this could be one of his most drastic formulations. Naming should be enough. As if it were a change of clothing that swathes and suffocates the adjectives.

And poetry, in the cold of January, is high summer to Ungaretti.

And amidst the sounds of war, the music of the weaponry, which is not the music expected at death, the words appear. Alone.

When Ungaretti has no ink and paper, which is often, he has to memorise the poems that assault him. So he walks through the trenches reciting in a low voice, and the soldiers and officials think he is praying or has gone slightly mad – if they are not all mad by now – or that he is repeating an order he must not forget.

For reasons of basic security, the trenches are dug not in a straight line but in a zigzag pattern that means you can never see further than ten metres along them. They weave back and forth, and even for a veteran soldier who has seen plenty of things, it is not an everyday sight to come across the poet walking with his head down, going over the words in order to ensure the poem doesn't escape. Ten metres, then he disappears.

In August 1916 he writes his poem 'The Beautiful Night', which ends:

Now I'm drunk
With universe.

Does the poet spare a thought for the Italian army postman, who risks his life to carry the letters from the front to their final destinations? In war, replies to letters are of the greatest importance when it comes to defeating the enemy: the soldier's spirit must remain whole and thereby give him reasons to continue the fight.

What would the postman do if he knew that one of the letters declares that things must be named without applying adjectives to them? Is this an official order? Are they fighting and giving their lives so language can cheat death?

Could this perhaps be the same postman who, once the war is over, takes the letters from Austrian soldiers imprisoned in northern Italy? There is one with an unusual address. The envelope is heavy, and reads: Trinity College, Cambridge. Inside is the manuscript of a book: *Tractatus Logico-Philosophicus*.

In a battle, the adrenaline often causes soldiers to see things in slow motion, but among these things are others that move at a terrifying speed: frantic rays of light that shoot from one point to another in a straight line like a meteor shower, sometimes seeming to form shapes that disappear again in an instant. Is this what Ungaretti claimed to have seen? Black holes appear too, as if the smoke of the bombs had formed an opening that leads to outer space. Starless voids, like a kind of magnetised womb that can only be glimpsed out of the corner of the eye (since looking at it directly causes death, according to those who had been at the front).

People who have experienced war also know that it is vital not to fall asleep in the snow. In the cold, falling asleep means freezing to death. In the battle you have to keep going, however much the adrenaline causes things to move in slow motion, and then, when everything has become glacial, these holes open up, real black holes.

Constellations, says Vonnegut. Like strands of white wool in the middle of the Arctic; taut, frozen, barely visible. Or rather, only the knots that hold them together are visible, and they look like stars. And the constellations go by one after the other at an incredible speed, as if on a journey towards planets where everything is one, where everything that has been left behind can be seen at the same time. And reduced to a haiku, to a word without adjectives.

But can nothing be heard there, in those holes?

No. It is the same silence of infinite space that terrified Pascal. No. Nothing is heard out there when everything stops and these fireflies appear, disinterested, immune to everything, as if contemplating a kind of pantomime.

Perhaps because he doesn't have the balls to commit suicide – as if suicide were like a round of golf – Ludwig

Wittgenstein enrols as a volunteer in the Austrian army soon after the start of the First World War. What's more, he asks to be sent to the frontline. This is a doubly unusual request because Ludwig is the son of one of the wealthiest and most cultured families in Europe, and naturally has the means to avoid such a fate. But fate is for big things: three of the seven children of Karl Wittgenstein have committed suicide, and the idea has been circling in Ludwig's head for some time. It is no joke. Indeed, Otto Weininger, a writer he greatly admires, especially for his book *Sex and Character*, shot himself in 1903. There are more than one million webpages about the author of the *Tractatus*. He wrote only two more books than Socrates. But these two books were enough to elevate the sort of mountain range where few climbers attempt to plant a flag. Two mountain ranges, in fact: one facing another across a gulf of twenty years. In between, a great valley of academics left stupefied, furious, stunned, open-mouthed.

During the Great War, Wittgenstein takes part in dangerous reconnaissance missions and at one point is hit by enemy fire. In war, he cares less about the defence of his country than about his self-control. He carries with him at all times a notebook in which he writes the notes that will come to form the *Tractatus*. The ideas that took Wittgenstein to war are soon exchanged for others. His diaries are unclear as to the reasons for this, but his biographers describe traumatic experiences. His social status and reserved character are mocked by his comrades. One night Wittgenstein enters enemy territory and lights a cigarette (probably the last one he smoked in his life). It is well known that you can take three puffs before a soldier blows your brains out: by the third drag the enemy has taken aim, and is ready to fire at the glowing point in the dark. The fireflies collide, the soldier is dead. Wittgenstein lights the cigarette and takes three long drags. Fireflies a shot away. Those were his risks.

The world is made up of facts, he says in his book, facts that are atoms, the smallest unit into which spoken reality can be divided. Language weaves meaning together like an invisible needle, linking these facts by means of the thread of its logic. In the trenches, Wittgenstein wants to reveal the limitations of language in order to reveal another reality that cannot be attained through thought.

To what extent is it possible to say something that makes sense (whether true or false)?

Military orders make sense, they demand obedience from those who hear them, they alter the trajectories of bodies and twist wills. The *Tractatus* could easily be read out in a martial tone. Yet the syllogisms it contains are not military orders, but rather a rigorous outpouring of ideas that test the prison of language.

Whereof we cannot speak, thereof we must remain silent, he wrote at the end of his book, from a prisoner of war camp in Italy in 1918.

More exactly: where we must remain silent, we can only *show*.

But since we also *are* language, as Basho understood before so many others, the key to the prison ought to be found in the haiku. It's like the principle behind vaccines: work together with the thing we wish to fight against.

The opposite of any order.

In November 1914, Wittgenstein wrote in his diary: 'It seems evident that the structure of the world must be capable of being described without using a single name.'

In the battle, at the beginning and at the end, is the word.

In 1916 Ungaretti wrote the poem 'Annihilation', later published in his collection *Joy*:

My heart showered fireflies
turning on and off
from green to green
I did decode.

And in 'May Night' he writes:

The sky crowns
the minarets
with garlands of little lights.

In the heat of battle, no one talks. There is only screaming. Everything is always for the first time.

The whispers, secretive words for the four or five who advance in the night; murmured haikus. There are no adjectives. Ungaretti carries binoculars and names what the moon allows him to see: a very large tree, rippling water, mortars.

And what lies outside the prison if the limits of the world and of language turn out to be one and the same?

Huddled one night alongside the body of a slain comrade, Ungaretti writes:

Never did I
so
cling to life

It forms part of the poem 'Vigil'.

Around the same date, Wittgenstein wrote in his notebook: 'Perhaps the proximity of death shall bring light to my life.'

Wittgenstein hears orders. He knows their meaning is to impose order on the meaninglessness of the war.

Ungaretti whispers. He orders things wordlessly in his nocturnal incursions behind enemy lines. He creates meaning, in order for the military advance to spread the chaos of blood and of fire.

The poet Lawrence Ferlinghetti was present at the Normandy landings. The last survivor of the beat generation. He wrote just one haiku, or rather he found it. American Haiku, he called it:

It's a bird,
It's a man,
It's... Superman!

The next note in Wittgenstein's blue notebook could equally be read as a haiku:

17997557
17997559
Prime numbers!

In one of the letters he sent to Bertrand Russell from the front, Wittgenstein wrote *tratactus* in place of *tractatus*.

A dyslexic twist that goes unnoticed by Russell, who was in prison for opposing the war.

Like nearly everyone who had been there, Wittgenstein never fully emerged from the trenches. He even continued to wear the uniform of Austria-Hungary long after the empire had ceased to exist.

In the trenches, the starry sky is the only place where the gaze can expand at will. Normally, the zigzag design permits a view of ten metres to either side; there is nothing to see to the rear, and to take a look at what's in front invites a shot to the head. As Austria's long-time ally, Italy also fights in zigzag trenches, against Austria.

Before and after the war, Wittgenstein sought out solitude and cold, which are different forms of slowness, in order to think better. Iceland, Norway on two occasions, a monastery.

The limits of Europe are the limits of language.

And then he travels to the beginnings of language: he takes up teaching at rural primary schools in Austria.

Wittgenstein is a tormented homosexual. Before the war he falls in love with an English student called David Pinsent. His love is silent. They live like kings in Iceland (Ludwig has not yet renounced his family's wealth). The war awaits them both upon their return from Reykjavik. In 1918 Pinsent dies in an accident in a military plane. Wittgenstein is struck dumb by the news. He dedicates the *Tractatus* to him and thinks about suicide.

In Norway, where he retreats to think, he has the Kant-like habit of leaving his cabin to walk every afternoon. Everything tends to be slower in the cold, until it reaches the most crystalline stillness, which is why people walk faster. The breath that freezes as soon as it leaves his mouth, the raw material with which the tongue forms words, or whatever remains of language, remnants surrounded by noise. And this thing whereof we cannot speak, Ludwig, is it this little mouth-ghost that surrounds our words in the cold? In Norway, in Iceland, in the trenches?

He resembles Séraphitüs, the character from Balzac's bizarre novel, who lives in northern Norway and is neither man nor woman, like the shamans who travel to the heaven of the hares in a trance.

In the extreme cold, words emerge stuttering. They pile up in the mouth and are expelled one by one, guillotined by the teeth. Words with a kind of dyslexia that goes unnoticed, like seedless grapes, like fireflies in the midday sun.

3. LAMBS

It was on a Sunday, of course, the day when what is highest is lowest, that the Brazilian priest Adelir de Carli, having administered holy communion, attached one thousand balloons filled with helium to a cushioned chair, strapped himself in with a seat belt and, when his altar boys released the anchors, flew up into the sky. As may be anticipated, this audacious act had a noble purpose: to raise money to build what was described as a lorry drivers' shrine. Strange as it may sound, a lorry drivers' shrine was needed in this city of Paranaguá, on a heavily-trafficked route between Curitiba and São Paulo. Before the faith of the drivers was won over by local beliefs of African ancestry, Adelir de Carli wanted to consecrate a kind of spiritual service station where the pumps delivered only the purest essences.

It's never very clear why breaking a record is supposed to generate cash. Spending three days swimming across the Arctic to save the pandas, for example. It seems the shouts of encouragement, the press coverage and the vigils of the NGOs translate all the nerves and sweat into clinking coins, clinking like bells, every passing day. The strange enthusiasm of people who bet on someone else's sacrifice for a few pennies. Indolent Guinness Christs and everyone's a winner. Fame, salvation, soothed consciences.

In any case, the parish priest of the lorry drivers, certain of winning publicity and cash for his shrine, tied himself to this huge cluster of balloons and a chair that in the pictures in the papers looks more like a kind of harness, and shot into the air like a Father Christmas who had lost his reindeer. He aimed to fly for up to twenty hours. After eight, nothing more was seen or heard of him.

The *orisha* spirits have taken him to the forest, or to the ocean, who knows, the lorry drivers whisper.

What we do know is that even if the Chinese invented everything, the Americans hold all the world records. The record for the longest balloon-powered flight is nineteen hours, held by a yankee from Ohio. The priest had managed four hours and fifteen minutes in a test run a few months earlier. The images on the news show him waving at his audience before the launch. There isn't much of an audience, to be honest. It's as if people had a premonition of the tragedy. He takes off into the sky at an alarming rate and disappears into the clouds. He had plenty of water and cereal bars with him. The last thing he was heard to say into his mobile phone was 'I need to contact the ground staff so they can tell me how to use the GPS. It's the only way I can give them my longitude and latitude so they know where I am.' Then silence.

Something doesn't make sense. How is it possible that he set off just like that, without even knowing how the GPS worked? Nobody jumps out of a plane without knowing where the ripcord on the parachute is. His planned means of descent was itself rather curious: popping the balloons one by one, pausing between each. The news reports gave no hint of advisors, engineers, physicists – some Brazilian incarnation of the Montgolfier brothers – who might have provided simple guidelines on how to handle such a singular vehicle.

The spirit blows where it wants and when it wants. What promised to be a gentle ride inland changed when the wind suddenly and without warning swung round to the west. Adelir de Carli intended to fly over the jungle, but ended up being taken out to sea. What began as Mary Poppins ended up as Captain Ahab.

Around the same time, in April 2008, newspapers reported that Pink Floyd's giant inflatable pig had escaped in the middle of a concert. It had gone on the stampede once before, when it was set free for the photos that appear on the disturbing cover of their 1976 album *Animals*. It landed fifty miles away, in Kent. They called it Algie and it accompanied them on all their tours. Wasn't the Devil meant to be a goat, Adelir de Carli asked himself when he saw the giant pig coming towards him. He would have preferred to have run into sheep or lambs, the lamb of God or some sacred cows falling down from heaven. Does the priest plummet to the ground or disappear into the sky? If he falls, his mouth opens wide with his scream and he runs out of air after less than a minute. Once his lungs are empty and he still hasn't reached the ground, does the body breathe in again or has the soul left it already? The mouth wide open like a cervical passage, expelling air from the blackness, the abyss of the body. *Abyssos*, in Greek, meaning bottomless. Your whole life, they say, flashes before your eyes in a moment, just like the body of the baby passes through the birth canal. The *aaaah!* as the final mantra and the cry of the mother as the first sound that is heard out there. From one abyss to another. But if, on the other hand, the priest continues to ascend unstoppably until his lungs are empty, does he scream? If so, when does the scream end? The horizon has become crescent-shaped, the senses are muddled, the perfume of saintliness permeates the balloons as the light fades. Up there, at such a great elevation, night doesn't fall. Instead, he climbs into the night. And, Adelir, this loss of consciousness, this breathing that becomes more and more laboured, wasn't this what the artist Marina Abramović was seeking with her partner Ulay in their performance *Breathing In/Breathing Out* in 1977? The mouths of Ulay and Marina sealed in a suicidal kiss; the oxygen moving from one body to another, becoming denser and slower until the carbon monoxide opens the doors to unconsciousness. At each performance, Marina Abramović reached states of consciousness that left her on the brink of death. Not unlike breaking a world record in order to save the pandas. But that is not the intention here. In another of her performances, she stands face-to-face with Ulay and they scream at each other for forty-five minutes until their voices are nothing but a thin whisper disappearing into a tunnel. It's called *AAA-AAA* and you can see it on the Internet. Voices giving up because there's no feeling to substantiate them. A dog doesn't end up hoarse from too much barking, nor a mother from too much weeping. But this is an expression without emotion, without substrate. A mantra that fades away, that's what *AAA-AAA* is. Or is it about adding sound to the mute cry of Munch? No, it's not that either. Because in *The Scream* the figure has its hands over its ears, which is where both fear and balance are located. The sky is red in Munch's *The Scream*, red is the wind-torn sky over Santa Catarina in Brazil, and the priest rises so high that his voice disappears, covering his ears as he goes, only to find out that God is deaf, the sky is black and the voice is a fine thread like those by which he is attached to the helium balloons. Did he meet Marina Abramović's grandfather up there, who – unlikely as it may sound – was the last saint of the Orthodox church? There's nothing about him online, but he almost certainly practised Hesychasm, the mystical union with God through regulated breathing and physical immobility – the closest

Christianity comes to yoga. And Adelir de Carli, bound to his chair, abandons the mantra *aaaah* and breathes thinner and thinner air. Silent mantras: even better. In another of Marina Abramović's performances she remains silent for hours and hours, like her grandfather and the saints of Mount Athos, in order to absorb all the energy present in the gallery in Copenhagen. And in *The House with the Ocean View* she places herself on show, ingesting nothing but water for a period of twelve days, in full view of all comers. The exhibition of an anchorite, with not even the cereal bars Adelir de Carli has with him as he climbs and climbs in his chair carried by balloons, like the lamb of God, in full view of no one, alone but pursued by the misgivings of half the planet, who don't know whether to laugh or cry about the whole affair. Does he stop screaming at some point, perhaps when he realises that the arrival of night doesn't shut the mouth that opened so wide when the sun disappeared below a horizon that is now curved like a dish? Does the priest look down? Does he get dizzy? Marina Abramović's grandfather, contemplating the view from the heights of Mount Athos, immobile, not lowering his gaze because with it the body too falls. Perhaps the priest committed suicide, unbuckling himself from the chair and casting himself into the void to die asphyxiated?

What do you mean, he didn't know how to work the GPS?

And nothing, but nothing on the Internet about Marina Abramović's grandfather.

It is 1987 and Primo Levi falls, tugged downwards by the gravity of the stairwell in his block of flats. Apparently, Levi suffered from vertigo. But how can it be that someone who has been thrown down as low as it is possible to go, who has lived in the abyss — and the abyss is not a place but a state of falling — could fall once more? The hole that opened up at Levi's feet, the void of the stairwell, is that Auschwitz? That night which cracked open one day and never closed again. Which silences those who were there. Voiceless, immobile, half-dead. The voice, if not a scream, is once again a fine thread and the deflating balloon. Nothing but carbon monoxide. But vertigo is not so much the fear of heights, of falling. Vertigo is about the irresistible power of the void, the fear of the void winning. It is the sirens of Ulysses and the ears unstopped. The angelic choirs that Levi must have heard calling from the darkened stairwell, the Nazi orders. And the hands cupping the ears. The lost balance. He fell four floors.

A child points to the sky above Rio de Janeiro: look, Grandpa, a satellite! His excitement escapes in a cry through his index finger. But no. It's not a satellite. It's the priest crossing the sky, his balloons lit up like miniature suns.

Around this time a report appears that puts an end to the mystery of the disappearance of Antoine de Saint-Exupéry. He had been shot down by a German fighter plane. The pilot says he would never have opened fire if he'd known it was the writer flying the enemy aircraft. When he realised beyond a shadow of a doubt what he'd done, he swore himself to silence on the matter. There must be a curse on the loose, because it's no simple thing to kill the Little Prince and carry on without a sense of guilt, for all the talk of anonymity and of just following orders.

It happened in Toulon, Horst Rippert began to recount to a French journalist. 'He was flying below me while I was on a reconnaissance mission over the sea. I saw his markings, manoeuvred myself behind him and shot him down.' During the Second World War, Rippert was a pilot with the Luftwaffe. 'If I'd known it was Saint-Exupéry, I would never have shot him down. We all read him when we were young. We loved his books,' he said, and the sadness still weighed on his face.

Many years after the war, the world learned that Saint-Exupéry disappeared on the 31st July 1944 while under-taking a reconnaissance mission ahead of the landings on the French Mediterranean coast. He'd taken off in a Lightning P38. With this information, it wasn't hard for Rippert to deduce that he was the one who'd shot him down. He never said anything to anyone, except to his wife one night while drunk, in the 1970s: I killed the Little Prince, I killed the Little Prince, he said, his voice cracked by the alcohol.

The Little Prince is a child without a balloon. He escaped his asteroid thanks to some wild birds. He travels wherever the winds in space carry him.

As for Adelir, the Brazilian priest, wasn't it suicide? How is it possible that he didn't know how the GPS worked?

That's what people say about Saint-Exupéry: that he was trying to commit suicide, or rather that, heedless to the call of vertigo, he was seeking assistance with a step he couldn't bring himself to take. At least that's what Bernard Mark, an aviation historian, believes.

What could have made him want to end his life after writing a book like *The Little Prince*? What do you see from such heights? The same things as Primo Levi saw from the abyss where he found himself? It's said that a week before he disappeared, Saint-Exupéry hinted at his suicidal intentions. In fact, even when he was flying over Turin, months before the events in Provence, he carried out a strange series of manoeuvres. The Germans failed to open fire, astonished by the 'indifference of the French pilot who stuck to his course even when he came within range of their guns'. 'Saint-Exupéry himself said that when he saw them approaching, he turned the rear-view mirror around and waited for them,' claims Bernard Mark. 'I never saw the pilot,' says Rippert, 'I never saw a parachute open.' 'Could he have got out?' At this, Rippert shrugs. He looks at the camera. 'Perhaps,' he says, 'perhaps he could have,' and he buries his face in his hands. He is over eighty years old. He looks like a child.

One night, Rippert's wife comes into his study. Rippert jumps. He thought she was having dinner with her friends. She begins to explain why she's back so soon (apparently one of her friends had been taken ill and the dinner had ended before it even began) when she notices that her husband's desk is covered with hundreds of drawings. All the drawings are of the same thing: lambs. Lambs of all shapes and sizes. Drawn and painted in pastel, oil, pencil, charcoal, ink. Hundreds of lambs. Rippert has been drawing them for years, ever since he realised he was the one who had killed Saint-Exupéry. He draws at least one lamb every night and adds it to his secret collection. Rippert's wife feels like Shelley Duvall in *The Shining* when she discovers that her husband Jack Torrance (Jack Nicholson) hasn't written any of the novel that was the reason he'd agreed to become caretaker of that Colorado hotel over the winter. Hundreds of pages covered with the same words, thousands of times: *All work and no play makes Jack a dull boy*. A mantra. In the same way, Rippert's wife realises at a glance that for years her husband has been drawing lambs under the Bavarian moon and silently hiding them away. Lambs that sometimes fade into silence, like Abramović's voiceless scream. Rippert runs out of ink, of paint, and his nocturnal lamb appears as a phantom, a mere outline, a blur of a body. Even so, Rippert puts it away without trying to retouch it later. That's how it was

made, and that's how it will stay. The lungs of Adelir de
Carli, high priest of the lorry drivers, without a drop of
oxygen left, far above. The void appears among the alveoli.
As if she had caught her husband with a secret lover,
Rippert's wife asks over and over again, shaking: what are
all these lambs? What does all this mean? She spreads the
pages across the desk. Drawings, watercolours, sketches.
Rippert says nothing. He is empty. They're just lambs, dear,
he says after a while, his eyes averted, his voice a thread
he ties to another balloon. What's wrong with drawing
lambs? Nothing, she replies. There's nothing wrong with
drawing one, or two, or thirty. But not hundreds of them.
Not hundreds. His wife is on the verge of tears. She is like
a slender crystal and the lambs begin to bleat like tenors.
Rippert raises his gaze, his eyes like glass. I just draw lambs,
dear.

Some time later, on the night when he was drunk
and defeated and he told her he'd killed the Little Prince,
his wife didn't think of the lambs for a second. What
do you mean, you killed the Little Prince? What Little
Prince? Saint-Exupéry. I killed Saint-Exupéry. Rippert has
newspaper clippings locked in his desk drawer that leave no
room for doubt.

A few years before the events off the coast of Provence,
Amelia Earhart had disappeared into the sky. A pioneer of
aviation in the United States, Amelia was probably one of
the most beautiful women in history. Many photographs
of her reveal her striking resemblance to the sculpture of
Queen Nefertiti. The full lips, the Cleopatra nose, a gaze
that's at once sweet and penetrating. Amelia also bore a
certain likeness to Charles Lindbergh, who made the first
solo transatlantic flight and was one of the most famous
men in the world in his day. The physical similarity between
the two was notable. To a certain extent this enhanced the

figure of Amelia, since Lindbergh was nothing other than the American Dream in physical form. Lindbergh: a Nazi, an anti-Semite, a superman who was not at all in favour of a war against Hitler. A hero whose child is kidnapped and murdered. An American tragedy. A suspect is found: a German immigrant by the name of Hauptmann. How will he defend himself before the jury? By drawing lambs and giving one lamb to each of them, one to the judge, and one to the newspaper's courtroom sketch artist.

The war has not yet broken out and Léon Werth, the friend of Saint-Exupéry to whom he dedicated *The Little Prince*, has forgotten how to draw lambs. He is in hiding and he's hungry and afraid, according to the dedication. Did Lindbergh know how to draw lambs, too? Were they like the ones that Hauptmann, the supposed murderer of his child, hands to the members of the jury before they condemn him to the electric chair? Why draw a lamb, Amelia Earhart would ask in the clouds; why not an eagle, a condor? Why a lamb if what is flying towards you is a pig? Adelir de Carli up in the skies listening to Pink Floyd, how is it possible you didn't foresee that a flock of birds like the ones that carried the Little Prince to Earth could peck at your balloons and you would fall, just as Amelia Earhart's aircraft supposedly fell, somewhere near Hawaii, the island where Lindbergh died? Supposedly, because nothing more was heard of her.

Lambs of God. A void that swallows everything. Like Cleopatra, the Little Prince seeks a voluntary death in a serpent's bite.

The high and the low: Auschwitz, a vertigo that silences, that takes the breath away, that empties the lungs. Lambs. Drawing lambs before the night opens its mouth in the mouth of our body. Drawing lambs: the only thing that saves us.

4. ENUMA ELISH

A very curious thing: nobody this century has produced more images than the iconoclastic Islamists who demolished the Twin Towers. The most famous of these images is without question that of the man falling headlong. At the other end of the lens is Richard Drew, a photographer who knows he's never going to win the Pulitzer for this. He has already taken another famous photograph: that of Robert Kennedy, just after he was killed by a bullet to the head. Spattered with blood, Drew ignores the cries of the senator's wife, Ethel, as she begs him not to take pictures of her husband. He finds the call of posterity more persuasive. Plenty of essays and novels have already dealt with the falling man. For a time, no one wanted to reveal his name, as if not doing so would thwart his definitive collision with the pavement. But since a journalist's shame is always up for grabs, tenacious enquiries shatter the limbo and there is no consolation to be had for anyone. His name can be found all over the Internet. His mother immediately knew that it was her son – blood ties correct myopia and long-sightedness alike – but didn't want it to be revealed.

Proper names, like all words, also have their reverse side. However, the crack that opens up when we pronounce them only exists for a couple of seconds every century, to exaggerate just a little. No one mispronounces their child's name, or their father's or their own. What would happen if we did? Isn't there a whiff of death in the air when a parent mispronounces their child's name? We're like nocturnal hares caught in the headlights when we hear it happen. It's almost physically impossible for a mother to mispronounce their child's name. And what you find there is the reverse of the person. The shadow acquires another dimension.

Suspended in the air, then, and dividing in two the tower that acts as backdrop. No one is going to speak his name. And if the mother's shock caused her to mispronounce it? Would this open up a crack through which he could disappear forever, straight to the space zoo of Tralfamadore? And if we were to misspell that as *Trafalmadore*, another door still would open and who knows where the man would end up.

The falling man is positioned exactly at the centre of the backdrop, with light on one side and shadow on the other. He appears to be dark-skinned, and the highest-resolution images show that he's wearing a pink shirt. He is falling headfirst, dividing what is from what is not, right at the line between light and shadow, at the midpoint, like his parents taught him, because in life all extremes are best avoided.

Beauty and terror come together, and this is the true horror of the photograph: its involuntary aesthetic qualities. How to avoid the visual judgment, to remove the subject and see only that someone has been caught there forever in pure form? I once read a poem that began *Daddy hung himself from a really beautiful tree.*

Two days before this leap, on the 9th of September 2001, the writer Jorge Barón Biza threw himself from a twelfth-floor balcony in the city of Cordoba in Argentina, one minute before the sun rose. He had spent the whole night listening to classical music, culminating in a strange combination of dissonant trumpets and saxophones at full volume which left his neighbour irritated and concerned.

'I was on the point of calling the police,' he told the paper *La Voz del Interior*.'Then the music stopped and there was silence, which was a huge relief.' Barón Biza falls and it's the last in the series of suicides enumerated on the dust jacket of his sole book, *The Desert and its Seed*, published in 1999. His father shot himself, and his mother and sister both threw themselves out of windows. His father, Raúl Barón Biza, was pretty crazy: he wrote pornographic novels and disfigured his second wife with sulphuric acid. His first wife was a Swiss actress who fell madly in love with him and came to live in Cordoba. She died when her private plane crashed, and her husband had a kind of Taj Mahal erected in her memory. He liked to tell people that priceless jewels were buried in its foundations.

Although no one saw Barón Biza fall, everyone saw his ascent. One single book was enough to carry him to great heights.

Meanwhile, what music was playing in his head? No one saw Barón Biza fall, despite the cover of his book making it quite clear it would be almost impossible for him to escape a fate that had taken his father, mother and sister. Is there something in the blood?

Is there something in language?

'I am writing this because it is the best way to get to know my siblings,' Wittgenstein says in a letter to Bertrand Russell.

Something in the blood? Primo Levi's grandfather killed himself. We also inherit the colour of our eyes from our grandparents.

How is it possible that no one saw Barón Biza fall?

One person's fall counts for everyone: the man falling headfirst from the Twin Towers is the only death actually shown in the media coverage. Or the only person shown under the spell of death, because he is in a state between one thing and the other. The photograph suggests he is no longer screaming. He is falling so fast that his lungs can no longer take in air.

Why on earth would you believe that Times Square gypsy saying you're going to kill yourself tomorrow, when Brenda's crazy about you and you've just been promoted to that office with the view of the whole of Manhattan?

And in Paranaguá everyone is hoping that Drew, the photographer of the falling man, will come to hunt that bright priest, so that instead of plummeting like Icarus he is captured in the most beautiful photograph in the world. One that puts death on hold, delaying the inevitable: an ID photo for a metaphysical bureaucracy. The most famous pictures in history show neither the dead nor the living, but those who are anonymous, on the threshold.

And so the lorry drivers went to collect Drew from São Paolo airport. They'd paid his American Airlines fare. Drew arrived at ten at night, but they didn't allow him time to recover from the trip. He could rest later, in a very nice hotel they had booked for him.

They take him to a headland on the first evening, and to a beach the second. He'd said he could stay for two days. The best hours of the day for glimpsing the priest are dawn and dusk, when the sun is still up but not dazzling. He climbs the headland together with a silent crowd. As the sun sets, hundreds of birds begin their deafening chatter.

Drew cannot distinguish the sounds of other animals. Are there monkeys? Tigers? He knows little of zoology, but imagines the jungle is home to such creatures.

They see shooting stars. The lorry drivers read omens into them. The atmosphere is celebratory. No one talks; all heads are turned to the sky, as if expecting rain. The official search for the priest has already been called off. The helicopters have all gone, though a private plane passes over every now and then, piloted by some Opus Dei follower seeking his own salvation by saving others, but to no avail. Nothing. The priest has vanished.

The next day they head down to the beach. Drew boards a small boat and they row out until the coast disappears. The silence is total.

Later, Drew will say that the whole thing felt like a kind of madness, and still does. But at that moment, waiting in the middle of the sea for a flying priest to drop out of the sky so he could take a photograph and save the man's soul, because he must be dead by now (mustn't he?), at that moment it seemed like the most truthful thing he had experienced in a long time. I felt, he told a newspaper, I felt like I was sat there before the truth, in that little boat watching the faces of the lorry drivers, who, like a pendulum, looked up at the sky and then down at me. When I found myself watching them, they gently motioned to me to keep pointing my camera at the sky. It began to get dark. The only photograph Drew could take was of his companions in the boat. Half-smiles, frank smiles. When night fell, once again there were shooting stars and then hundreds of stars filled the sky, the ones the lights of the city drown out as soon as they emerge. Impossible to see the priest. Satellites could be made out, craft circling the Earth. Isn't it possible that the priest is one of those lights? Holiness fills bodies with light, and so it must be with the balloons as well. A lighthouse for nocturnal birds, Adelir de Carli, lord of the lorry drivers, master of the migratory birds, eternal child with your multi-coloured balloons, you drift ever further from the planet, airless, on your way to who knows where.

Beautiful, intrepid, vertiginous, Miriam Stefford shares a number of attributes with Amelia Earhart. A Swiss actress turned pilot, she crashed in San Juan, Argentina, in 1931. In her memory, her husband, Barón Biza senior, built the largest mausoleum in the country in the city of Cordoba. An aeroplane wing sticking out of the ground, more than 80 metres high, through which a cross of light is projected that strikes the woman's coffin. Who knows what tragedies her death saved her from. Only guilt or pain – or equal parts of both – could justify such a vast quantity of reinforced concrete. It's always been said that he knew Miriam was cheating on him with her flying instructor, and saw to it that the aircraft had a slight mechanical fault. Miriam's jewels are buried beneath the mausoleum. Naturally, there's a curse waiting for anyone who tries to desecrate the tomb. Because everything about the life of this man was excessive. A man who ended up shooting himself after he had disfigured his second wife with acid. And she in turn, once her face had been fixed up as best as possible, threw herself out of a window.

Miriam had appeared in just three movies, all of which had predictable titles. One example is enough: *Hand of Aces*. Like Amelia, she wanted to link Argentina and the United States in one triumphant flight. She had to content herself with reaching the fourteen provincial capitals of Argentina, as they were at the time.

Her plane came down in the Valley of the Moon, in the northern province of San Juan.

Drew bids farewell to the lorry drivers in São Paolo airport. They take a few final pictures. He's one of the last to take his seat. Whenever he flies, he's struck by the same feeling of impossibility as the aeroplane takes off. The lights of São Paolo expand endlessly before him. His face is reflected in the window. From outside, his astonished portrait can be seen, dotted with yellow, white and red circles.

Before the sun emerges above the horizon, Barón Biza throws himself from the window. A final race, to reach the ground before the first point of gold appears. To swallow this point with his mouth full of the last sounds he makes. What's the pitch of his final cry? It's like a train disappearing into the distance. The mouth wide open so as the body falls it fills up with light.

5. TINNITUS

Around the same time the priest disappeared, the newspapers were reporting that the Chinese government had decided its space agency would send a philosopher on its next mission, to reflect on the experience of leaving the planet. Chinese philosophy takes a different approach to the inquiries of its Western cousin. Indeed, it only asks questions to which the answers are already known. If we think about it, that's what wisdom is, is it not? Obtaining answers without asking anything. Should we be expecting a haiku of some kind from this philosopher upon his return? Lao Tze knew many things without ever having left his position in the court of the emperor. When he retired to the forest, never to return, a palace guard, having heard of his wisdom, asked him to write down everything he knew for posterity. Lao Tze expounded his knowledge in five thousand Chinese characters, which is why his book, the *Tao Te Ching*, is also known as the *Five Thousand Character Classic*.

The Chinese Committee of Human Sciences and Philosophy announces the names of the three philosophers shortlisted for the voyage. Deng Jigme, Zhang Yun and Li Xiannian. Names that mean nothing on this side of the world and perhaps not much on the other side either, where they have more pressing concerns. Three professors. One wins, the other two console themselves with their media prominence, expanded CVs and material for further reflection.

The philosophers all know each other, of course, but they're not what you might call friends. It's likely that Xiannian and Jigme have a greater degree of affinity from time spent together at conferences. More than one book has compiled their essays. But outside the academic world, they have little in common.

The news of the winner reaches the press the day after the philosophers themselves learn that it is Zhang Yun.

The press are up all night wondering what on earth to ask him.

The matter went no further than a brief article, something for the Sunday colour supplement. The story would only take off with the launch of the rocket.

What do you expect to find up there? was one question. *Do you believe in God?* was another (really).

Zhang Yun lives in the suburbs of Shanghai, two blocks from the train line. Some afternoons he walks along the tracks with his seven-year-old son. They balance on the rails, seeing who falls off first. Their arms outstretched, crucified. The trick is not to look at where the foot needs to go but rather to gaze into the distance, to where the rails finally meet: infinity. If the sole of the foot is set down lightly, at an angle of almost forty-five degrees, and only briefly, as if the rail were hot, it's easy to keep your balance. It is concentrating too hard that makes you fall. It's getting late, Zhang Yun tells his son, who wants to carry on a bit longer. In the distance, a train whistle can be heard. The father turns around. It is the opposite of the lightning bolt: first the sound, then the image. It's still far away.

In his media interviews, Sun Ra put things in black and white: he had arrived from outer space to save the world with his music. In case any doubts remained, and for anyone who wanted to understand the sacramental nature of the matter, there was the 1974 film *Space is the Place*. Sometimes he said he came from Saturn. Other times, from an unknown planet beyond the solar system, which gave rise to the origins of his musical ideas. That's where he'd heard them. That's right. Yes. On that planet. In fact, very little information is available about his birth, if we ignore the record in the Library of Congress, which could easily be a fake. His most popular composition is 'Pink Elephants on Parade'. You can see and hear it in the Disney film *Dumbo*.

Sun Ra never fully explained how he reached our planet from Saturn or wherever he came from. He simply declared that he was 'compelled to be here, so anything I do for this planet is because the Master-Creator of the Universe is making me do it. I am of another dimension. I am on this planet because people need me.'

With the Solar Arkestra – previously known as the Solar Myth Arkestra, Myth Science Arkestra and Omniverse Arkestra – he recorded countless albums. The covers are, quite simply, demented. The music too, but in a different way: it's a mixture of big band, hard bop, psyche-delia, Pink Floyd-style space sounds, primitivism and a fascinating etcetera. He was also a pioneer in combining the music with his attire, and his band, which toured the planet continually, was accompanied by a tailor who did an excellent job of blending priestly Egyptian robes with metallic space suits like the ones in 50s B-movies. Somewhere between Ed Wood and Anubis. The band liked to play among the audience, with the saxophone players whirling like dervishes and Sun at the piano while conducting everyone else, his arms twirling as they marked the rhythm in a cocktail of sounds impossible to distin-guish one from the other. The saxes reached places they had never gone before, the rhythm a crazed metronome always on the point of shaking itself apart. The first-rank musicians included the brilliant saxophonist John Gilmore, Sun's right hand for almost forty years. Gilmore died two months after Sun himself departed on his final journey to the planet where, they say, music is composed by playing all the notes at the same time rather than in sequence. The changes in volume are the only sign that something is being played.

The train whistles again. A beam of sound that needs a prism to refract it into the seven musical notes.

On the track, Yun thinks: the tone of the telephone, the mobile phone, the buzz of the computer, domestic appliances... aren't they all just one single vibration?

Wasn't that how Kubrick conceived the sound of the black monolith in *2001: A Space Odyssey*?

Listen, Sun Ra says in the middle of a maelstrom of sound at Filmore's, Chicago. Listen carefully to the musical melody that has formed: we're playing our song.

On the track, Yun thinks: this sound is not created by bringing together what is separate. No, that's it! It is the white noise, all the domestic sounds that regiment and give orders to the body: get up, walk, run, lie down, stop.

It is the noise that the army of Sun Ra valiantly battles against in order to save the world. To put an end to the dictatorship of sounds that form a mesh protecting us from nature.

On the track, Yun thinks: who determines the noise that electrical equipment makes?

Sun Ra and his orchestra respond to the question 'Is this life?' with a five-minute laughing fit on the track 'Neptune', found on the album *Discipline 27-II*.

Yun walks on, balancing atop the rail with his son. Up there, in orbit, the sense of balance disappears and is replaced by a feeling of continuous free fall, even as the spacecraft is flying through the Milky Way. Space sickness, they call it, and it can give rise to optical illusions as well as nausea.

The philosopher prepares for months. But there is something soft in him. Even the military-trained astronauts suffer from space sickness.

One of the organs in the internal ear that it affects is the cochlea, which is spiral-shaped like all the best galaxies, and is where our sense of balance is located.

And curiously enough, space sickness, this sense of falling, is like descending into a giant, endless snail shell. A nautilus.

And around the periphery of the cochlea is where tinnitus takes hold, that persistent high sound, a whistle, white noise, a telephone no one ever answers, a train in the distance, tiny bells.

And the galaxies like a giant maelstrom.

A skein of stars.

And as soon as he's in orbit, our philosopher will see flashing lights. Space fireflies, phosphorescent globes. They won't be what Captain Dave Bowman saw in *2001*, those gleaming tongues of light from infinity. The philosopher will know very well when he is hallucinating.

Tinnitus has different nuances and changes in volume. A single sustained note, as if suspended, without the sense of falling. An equilibrium is reached, achieved by this sound that seems to come from the depths of the ear, tracing back the labyrinth of the cochlea to the depths of the most distant galaxies. Like a stave in the key of sol.

In 2001, German performance artist Wolfgang Flatz threw a cow from a helicopter. A Friesian, like the cow on the cover of the Pink Floyd album *Atom Heart Mother*, a dead, disembowelled cow with fireworks inside so it would explode in a thousand pieces over central Berlin. Mincemeat for all. The cow was dropped from a helicopter at a height of about 130 feet. It fell in the yard of a cultural centre in the fashionable district of Prenzlauer Berg. Meanwhile, Flatz hung from a crane with his arms outstretched like the Vitruvian man, which is a mathematical crucifixion if we think about it: a happy agreement between science and religion in the minds of Vitruvius, Da Vinci and a few others during the Renaissance.

It could also illustrate how reason crucifies man. Covered in blood, perhaps that of the cow killed especially for the performance. Flatz's stated intentions are pretty dull: *Fleisch* – the title of the piece – is supposed to question the relationship between man and the flesh, his body, his fears… Sometimes it's better not to let artists talk about their work.

But we were discussing the music of the spheres. A music that Wolfgang Flatz was seeking in an earlier performance – more reminiscent of those of Marina Abramović – when he hung himself upside down inside a kind of bell, with his head as the clapper. As he was swung from side to side, his head began to ring the bell. A gong mantra that resonates inside, like those Sun Ra played with his Arkestra. It lasted twenty minutes. Flatz swings from one side to the other of the bell, until his own head starts to ring. When this happens, when his own brainpan is nothing but a soundboard, Flatz falls unconscious, the bell ceases to ring, or at least is no longer heard, because he has taken the sounds inside him and they have taken him far away, beyond the solar system.

Zhang Yun wants to take the train's whistle with him in the same way. The white noise.

Sun Ra has no legal birth certificate. The only document accrediting his existence is the one in the Library of Congress which states he landed in Alabama. His passport gives his legal name as Le Sony'r Ra. In *Space is the Place* – a film near impossible to get hold of – directed by John Coney, Sun Ra arrives from Saturn on a craft powered by jazz music to save the black race from the control of the Overseer, an ally of NASA and the FBI, by playing him at cards.

Sun Ra found it difficult to fire a musician he wasn't getting along with. His usual modus operandi was simply to abandon them wherever the band was playing at the time. More than one diplomatic incident was caused by a saxophonist or percussionist left behind in some exotic country like Finland, India or Egypt. The baritone sax player Pepper Fleming joined the band very young. He was no musical genius, and Sun Ra eventually lost patience with his overly timid playing. That is to say, the band decided to split from him and head off to other planets, leaving the poor Christian in the land of the pharaohs with nothing more than a suitcase containing his sax and a change of clothing. He woke up very late, he recounts in an interview. In the hotel lobby they told him the band had checked out and were probably at the airport already. Fleming leapt into a taxi for a swift but fruitless ride. *Casablanca*: Fleming embracing the taxi driver as the plane takes off. It could be the beginning of a beautiful friendship, or a diplomatic wrangle. Pepper Fleming became a successful session musician, and you can appreciate his talents on a couple of tracks by The Carpenters.

The train whistles once more, closer this time. Yun tries to distinguish nuances in the sound, and yes, it seems there are nuances. In his crucifixion posture, walking along the endless rail, he draws level with his son and tries to touch his fingers. His son protests because it throws him off balance. Yun loses balance too and steps off the rail first. They start again and try to walk holding hands, but can barely reach each other's fingertips.

The most awful thing on 11th September 2001 was hearing the sound of the people falling. If you saw the body falling, you didn't hear the sound. And the other way around.

Prisms. Up there, won't we be prisms, the philosopher asks himself on the train tracks.

A dog joins the procession, lets out a bark that's more instinctive than anything else and snuffles among the stones between the rails. Yun's son picks up a stick and throws it as far as he can. The dog ignores him. Another whistle: the train is closer still. Yun turns. The train is approaching around the bend. He tells his son to step off the rails. The dog listlessly pads away. They get down from the tracks. The son takes his father's hand, and they move further back and watch the train draw nearer. His son asks, can you see the Great Wall from space? Along the Great Wall, ten million Chinese people are buried. The biggest cemetery in the world. No manmade structures can be seen from space. Yes, Yun replies, I'm going to see the Great Wall.

Two minutes later the train goes by. The engine driver raises his arm to greet the boy, and the boy looks up at his father, laughs and waves back. Some of the passengers looking out of the windows wave at them too. The train disappears into the distance, running along those parallel tracks that, strictly speaking, should only be possible in theory. A final whistle that persists in Yun's ears as he watches the carriages and knows there is a shore to be reached, but that the ocean he has to traverse is not one you can cross by swimming.

Wolfgang Flatz never fully recovered from his performance with the bell.

Sun Ra's orchestra lived in a commune. Their terrestrial base was in Philadelphia, but they toured the world to 'express the infinite and resolve cosmic equations on a musical plane'.

Any of the three shortlisted philosophers could have made the journey. There was a questionnaire, an interview, and physical and psychological tests. All to be expected. Some disconcerting questions: what is your favourite colour? What music do you listen to? Obvious answers: blue, red, green, Bach.

Yun knows that outside the spacecraft the temperature can reach 270 degrees below zero. Is this the cold of the Void? Does something like that really exist? The Void, Nothingness. Or is it the cold of the lines, the weave of waves and particles that constitute radio waves and everything else?

Is this the Tao?

How would Sun Ra have drawn a lamb? What is the lamb of the Egyptian gods? The truth is, the Little Prince causes people to draw lambs, but he never drew a single one himself. How could he have done? And does Adelir de Carli continue to ascend, has he fallen or has he been rescued by the orchestra of Sun Ra?

The absence of air makes sound impossible in space.

6. BUBBLES

The bravest man in the world was the son of a carpenter and a milkmaid. Like the animals, he knew only what he had to know and that was enough for him to reach where no one had been before, so high did he fly.

It's a well-known line: there are no atheists in foxholes. God, like fireflies, only shines in the darkness, wrote Schopenhauer. In the trenches, the only light is that of enemy fire. Up there in space, where the darkness is total, travelling at over 16,500 miles per hour in a tiny craft that will reach a temperature of 1,000 degrees Celsius when it re-enters the atmosphere, with no computer to control the descent, Yuri Gagarin declares, without ceremony, in a firm voice despite being curled up in a near-foetal position, *I see no God up here*. That's what you call having balls.

Yuri Gagarin was chosen from among 3,000 candidates to make the first manned voyage outside the Earth's atmosphere. The son of a milkmaid and a carpenter upholds the spirit of socialism better than one whose father is a teacher and has a foreign-sounding name: Gherman Titov misses out after two tie-breaks.

Upon his return there will be commemorative stamps, town squares, parks, chemical elements, walls. All in his name and charged to the account of the Russian state.

A journey of one hour and forty-eight minutes around the Earth is enough to secure his place in the memory of humankind. A 40-metre statue of him stands in Moscow. The titanium sculpture resembles a rocket-man. A superhero in the land of equals. There's a sculpture of his head on Cosmonauts' Alley, also in Moscow.

Yuri Gagarin's capsule landed in Tajtarova, Siberia. A peasant woman saw his parachute descend from just 200 metres away. Open-mouthed, she approaches him and asks if he has come from heaven. Certainly I have, Gagarin replies with his famous smile. This anecdote was obligatory reading in Russian schools until at least 1989.

Have you seen my Ivan? The peasant woman asks. (We have left the printed page behind.) Gagarin stares at her incredulously. Ivan?

Yes, my Ivan. He froze to death in Kolyma. Have you seen him? Have you seen my Ivan?

Gagarin knows the answer but remains silent.

The rescue team is still far away. The peasant woman takes him to her home, a crude cabin built to tolerate all the cold of Siberia. It smells of cabbage. Steam rises from cooking pots. Gagarin sits down at the table. There are three hard wooden chairs. The woman pours him a vodka. Yuri Gagarin doesn't know this will be the first of many glasses. If you go back up to heaven, take this coat to Ivan. The woman hands him a felt jacket.

Yuri Gagarin's death is shrouded in mystery. He dies without knowing that man will reach the moon just one year later. On 27th March 1968 he crashes his Mig 15 fighter plane not far from Moscow. Speculation about the accident mentions turbulence, mechanical failure, human error, alcohol.

Can you hear that band playing? It's the Glenn Miller orchestra on their European tour. Music to make the G.I.s feel at home as they shoot at Germans like they do at deer in Oregon, wild ducks in Arkansas and blacks in Alabama. A black German would be the Holy Grail, more than one of them thinks (yee-haw!).

Glenn Miller writes nothing but hits, conducts an all-white jazz band and plays the trombone; it's not long until his aeroplane will be lost for ever over the English Channel, establishing him once and for all as a true American hero. Nine years later, the ups and downs of his life – a rather bland one, despite all the patriotic activity – will be made into a movie. The real American squad is his orchestra, taking its feel-good mood to all the fronts; an optimistic syncopation, quite unlike the martial music wars tend to impose. As the band plays their serenades by moonlight, the soldiers dance through their battles, dodging the German bullets with a vigorous grace. Basho's willows. Among the soldiers listening to the music and howling like wolves that night in a barracks on the outskirts of London are many black G.I.s. One of them, quiet as a sheep, asks himself why he isn't up there, on the stage, if he can play far better than all those white guys put together. Why am I sat here with a gun in my lap? There's something unfair going on. An inner voice he can only just hear tells Pepper Fleming to be patient, there's still a long wait before Sun Ra's ship lands in Cleveland and takes him on tour to save the world with his tenor sax solos. Fifteen years, at least.

Tonight, friends, tonight we're celebrating: it's Glenn Miller's last concert in London. Afterwards he'll head to a brothel and be stabbed as he leaves, according to some; according to others, he'll be interned in hospital in the morning due to his advanced lung cancer; in the afternoon he'll leave for France and the plane will never arrive, according to posterity, and nothing will be known of him or the crew again. Musician, pilot and co-pilot swallowed up by a sea as calm as a mirror. Some say the plane came spiralling down after being hit by the English themselves, who, after an unsuccessful raid on the Germans, have to drop their bombs in the sea. One of them strikes Miller's plane. Miller hits the water and becomes food for the fishes, if we're to believe this story. What's unquestionable is that the aeroplane was never seen again. And because every country needs its heroes, it's not hard to imagine Miller playing his trombone as the plane comes down in the Channel. Three people and a trombone floating in the submerged cabin. Inside the body of the instrument, a trapped bubble of air contains Miller's last cry, like the amber that encloses Jurassic mosquitoes. Tangled inside the trombone, the cry needn't wait for a fish to find its way into the tubes or give a good blow on the mouthpiece: the increasing water pressure causes the bubble to emerge slowly, elongated; a silent cry, like the head of a foetus that has to break the amniotic sac and traverse the birth canal. But here the sac doesn't break until the last moment. The ocean is the infinite womb where the baby floats in the final scene of *2001: A Space Odyssey*. The baby, or rather the foetus, travels through space towards our planet, bringing about, depending on our interpretation, the most advanced stages of progress in order to establish a new humanity. An evolutionary leap, if this is how we are to understand the purpose of the famous black monolith that appears intermittently in the film. A fisher king, perhaps; the foetus, I mean, which ends up being eaten by the others, by its own creation. No, this wasn't Kubrick's idea in the film. However, the baby isn't like all the other foetuses, which only know the single-chord soundtrack of their mother's heart. The space baby only perceives the interminable hum of the monolith; its sun is elsewhere. Meanwhile, at this moment on Earth there must be some 60 million foetuses swimming in the timeless ocean inside their mothers, hearing the beat of an invisible red sun that communicates everything to them without language. But the baby arriving from space brings with it the melodies of Tralfamadore enclosed in the floating sac, a transparent balloon. Few will understand it. Below, in the ocean, the bubble has left Miller's trombone and almost reached the surface. And when it bursts, where will the freed cry go; that note open to all melodies, pure vibration seeking an ear to receive it? The wave is still silence. Silent too is the space baby in the warm uterus that protects it from the 270 degrees below zero out there. Will the icy needles of space abort its mission? Kubrick had already ended his previous film, *Dr Strangelove*, with a character falling to Earth: in the final scene, Major Kong mounts the atomic bomb in the aircraft hold and straddles it like a horse. While we're about it, is he not one of the horsemen of the Apocalypse? He descends, whooping like a good Texas cowboy, and his voice is all we hear; there's no background music, just a voice that gulps in air a couple of times because Major Kong doesn't think for a moment that this is how you die. In fact, he feels more alive than ever as he plummets with the bomb between his legs.

Also plunging with its atomic load, a year before the attack on the Twin Towers, is the Russian submarine *Kursk*, in the Barents Sea. It was blessed by an Orthodox priest in 1995. An outer shell of nickel-chrome steel: an underwater Titanic. The resurgence of Russia after the fall of the wall, its pride intact. When all the doors have been closed and the windows shuttered, the danger crouches within: a gas with an impossible-to-pronounce name leaks through the rust in a torpedo, which when fired produces an explosion. Firing practice with a dummy torpedo, that's all it took. A simple periodic table would have fixed it. Four compartments are flooded with the speed of a karate kick. The nuclear reactors are in the fifth. Did the priest do the right thing in blessing it? God is always found in excuses. The submarine sinks to the seabed. It takes sixteen days for the navy to acknowledge the tragedy and ask for international help. Inside, a number of sailors have survived inside a giant bubble of compressed air that is used up as it passes through their lungs. The sailors are in the dark. They are believed to have survived for six days. A weak, monotonous radio signal reaches them. Then, when the inevitable has been accepted, the pulse slows, nothing is expected to interrupt the monotonous sound from the radio, and eventually it stops and no one notices. Someone coughs, and later they all cough. Nothing. The sailors' voices have disappeared from their throats. They stopped singing long ago, then they stopped weeping, and finally they stop talking. They shift around, curl up, the knees and chin meet the chest.

Have you seen my Ivan up there? The peasant woman asks again and Gagarin takes the felt jacket she's holding out to him. Sometimes he comes, she says. In winter he comes through the tunnels. Yuri Gagarin knows just what she's talking about. When the cold goes beyond thirty-five degrees below zero, the air becomes so thick that it seems like a curtain of luminous fog, the frozen breath from a giant mouth, or the words of the winter gods frozen in suspense. Walking through this icy, phosphorescent landscape people carve out tunnels with their bodies. Ryszard Kapuściński describes the phenomenon in his book *Imperium*: 'The corridor has the shape of that person's silhouette. The person passes, but the corridor remains, immobile in the mist.'

I haven't seen my Ivan but I have seen his silhouette in the winter, he walks through the village but he never makes it home. He's lost. Ivan got lost. Gagarin pours himself more vodka. There's a crucifix on the sideboard.

The peasant woman hasn't told him her name. She wears a black handkerchief tied around her head and a grease-stained apron. Within an hour, the rescue team has arrived. The woman thinks they've come to take him back up to heaven. Yuri Gagarin kisses her on the forehead. He is exultant, having returned safe and sound from his voyage. Once he has left, the peasant woman notices that the man who fell from the sky has forgotten the felt jacket for her son. She smiles and cries at the same time. She wipes her hands on her apron, as if they were wet. Which ears will her weeping reach as it traverses the corridors of winter? It might be heard as far away as Kolyma.

Where will this bubble that emerged from the sea to become sound end up? Which ear will it reach, the final cry of this man who created the happiest and most joyful soundtrack to the grimmest years of the century?

And the whole affair comes to an end when the Americans drop the two bombs. In *Dr Strangelove*, as the atomic bombs are exploding before the credits roll, we hear Vera Lynn singing 'We'll Meet Again', the most famous song of the Second World War. As far as we know, it was never recorded or performed by the Glenn Miller Orchestra.

The U.S. army returns to the streets of New York. They parade down Fifth Avenue as ticker tape is thrown from the buildings, amidst rejoicing, laughter, kisses for the soldiers. All the orchestra's musicians have made it home, apart from Glenn himself, who will never see the paper streaming from the buildings, and will instead continue to fall endlessly into the English Channel, holding his trombone, in which a final note, the last cry, has been trapped.

At last the bubble reaches the surface, bursts and heads straight upwards until it's caught in mid-flight by a seagull. The bird feels a slight vibration, and carries it away to some cliff ledge where it takes refuge before nightfall.

7. LIGHTNING BUGS

Laika the dog was launched into space in November 1957 from the Baikonur base. Today, we know that she didn't survive the two weeks originally claimed; instead, seven hours after leaving the Earth, the heat of the spacecraft together with the violent stress ended her life. Over those fourteen days, people in rural areas would gather at night to watch her pass overhead, despite the extreme cold. For those with good eyesight it was hard to mistake her: only two satellites were in orbit at that time. As they watched, the farmers lit fires and tossed scraps of meat into the flames, the bones slowly scorching to black. Fourteen days, no less, for a stray dog found by an official from the aeronautics authority and who only needed two months of training to achieve eternal fame. For fourteen days, the dog traversed the clear night skies, greeted with shouts of jubilation and toasted with vodka.

The sun hits the summit of Everest. The climber is wearing an oxygen mask; his right hand raises a string of flags that can't be made out, but everyone knows that one of them is British. The photograph looks like a prayer card. Contrary to popular belief, it does not show Edmund Hillary, the first man to reach the peak of the world's highest mountain. Hillary is the one taking the photograph, and the climber is his assistant, Tensing Norgay, a humble Sherpa who, in gratitude to the gods of Chomolungma – the Tibetan name of Everest – dug a little hole at the peak and left an offering of chocolates, sweets and biscuits. Edmund Hillary was six foot six and his face appears on banknotes in New Zealand.

The man in the brown jacket who appears in the background of the cover of *Abbey Road*, standing on the pavement, has been identified by many as Pete Best, the Beatles' first drummer, who had been sacked from the band and was working as a civil servant. In fact, the band's manager, George Martin, has said the man is one Bob Ferry, or Perry, or something like that, who had stopped to look back at the Fab Four crossing the street for the photograph. Perry or Ferry turned up several times at the offices of the band's label to find out whether he appeared in the photograph or not, because at the moment the shutter clicked he was emerging from his lover's house, an address his wife already had her suspicions about.

Meanwhile, there are plenty of Englishmen who claim to be the surprised-looking man in brown.

While Neil Armstrong and Buzz Aldrin walked the lunar surface, Michael Collins stayed at the controls of the Columbia module, orbiting the moon at a height of exactly sixty-nine miles. They always knew one of the three astronauts would not descend to the moon's surface. The man who remains is the most important member of the expedition because he makes sure they all get back safely. But no rationalisation, nor even the arms of his wife Jodie, can console Collins.

The most famous photograph of Neil Armstrong on the moon is the photograph of Buzz Aldrin. Armstrong took it, and his image appears reflected in his companion's visor.

8. FIREFLIES

In humans and animals alike, a survival mechanism means the gaze always focuses on anything that's moving. An involuntary spasm inscribed in the genes. Speed means either danger or food: biology doesn't offer many more options. This is why it is very hard to carry on a serious conversation if a television is playing nearby: the pupils are drawn directly to the screen.

Who would have been the first to look up to the night sky without seeking anything at all, not even tranquillity? Free of questions, just standing quietly, in a state of total defencelessness, a rock-like innocence. Why would they have done such a thing? Eyes immune to the shooting stars, the comets and other points of light. A virgin pupil of metaphysics.

No animal gazes at the sky. That's why the sky, according to the shamans, is always full of animals.

There is a giant, unalterable and illegible haiku above our heads every night. A haiku that moves with the slowness of honey, as if waiting for someone able to catch it.

A story that rests on itself, a vault carved with ribbing of invisible ice, which ends up illuminating those who manage to read it.

An untranslatable story. Because, of course, it's not a story. Or a poem.

And it's written in all languages at once. All past and future languages, meaning that only a baby can read it. But babies don't look at the stars. At night, they sleep.

Now we come to think about it, it's enough to raise our heads to the sky for our mouths to fall open, as if the body already knew. Something like an ancestral memory. Then those who manage to read the haiku open their mouths even wider, and if something comes out it's in the form of a shout, a yell, a howl, until the lungs are empty.

Nothing that makes much sense. Like the stars an astronomer observes.

And all the fireflies that cry out when they manage to read the haiku do so tuned to the same frequency, which is not the usual La 440 Hz but rather La 439 Hz. This is because it's a prime number, and hard to obtain in a laboratory.

Very infrequently, a haiku hunter appears.

That's why we have to make do with the stories of these fireflies or lightning bugs that were never fully able to light up. Either they were consumed very quickly, or they never reached boiling point. Perhaps it's better for them this way. Warm embers.

And some stories remain in the inkwell, like that of Captain Servet, who in the Battle of the Marne shouted a mispronounced order – what word did he use? – and opened up a black hole in the middle of the combat, his battalion never to be seen again. There's another version of events: the soldiers returned when the war had ended saying they'd come from a place full of animals, and none of them were laughing.

No one stops shivering when the cold inscribes the names of their children in their bones.

After all, if we stop to think, the stars have been fleeing from us from the very beginning. Every night they're further away, though they give the impression of being in the same place.

But we shouldn't feel lonely as a result.

No. Not at all.

As long as there's a fire there will be a story waiting to be told. And then we'll open our mouths wide and swallow all that we can of the night.

And, for the first time, the same song will begin.

APPENDIX

The following people appearing in this book have an asteroid named after them:

Glenn Miller
Kurt Vonnegut
Amelia Earhart
Antoine de Saint-Exupéry
Yuri Gagarin
Bertrand Russell
Stanley Kubrick
Neil Armstrong
Buzz Aldrin
Michael Collins
Jürgen Habermas
Edmund Hillary

Pink Floyd, Lao Tze, Glenn Gould, Pascal, Jackson Pollock, Balzac, Schopenhauer and Bach, who are mentioned in passing in the text, also have their own asteroids.

Asteroid number 12,477 is called Haiku.

ACKNOWLEDGEMENTS

To Guillermo Martínez, for his selfless generosity, which permitted the ideal conditions for writing of this book.

To Apexart Curatorial Program and its director, Steve Rand, for a magnificent residency in New York.

A NOTE ON THE TEXT

Charco Press has reproduced the following with the generous permission of the relevant publishers and/or translators:

The quote from *Slaughterhouse-Five* by Kurt Vonnegut on p. 13 is from the following edition: Dell Publishing & Co., 1969, p. 76.

The verses 'My heart showered fireflies, turning on and off, from green to green, I did' and 'Never did I /so / cling to life' from the poem 'Annihilation' by Giuseppe Ungaretti come from *A Major Selection of the Poetry of Giuseppe Ungaretti* (Exile Editions, 1997), trans. Diego Bastianutti, p. 57. Permission granted by Exile Editions.

The verses 'Now I'm drunk / With universe' from the poem 'The Beautiful Night' by Giuseppe Ungaretti come from *Three Modern Italian Poets: Saba, Ungaretti, Montale* by Joseph Cary (University of Chicago Press, 1993), p. 156. Permission granted by University of Chicago Press.

The quote by Ryszard Kapuscinski on p. 77 is from *Imperium* (Granta Books, 1994), trans. Klara Glowczewska, p. 182.

TRANSLATOR'S NOTE

The original title of this novel is *Bellas Artes*, which means 'Fine Arts'. Dubious about whether such a title would attract attention, as the first book to be published by a hitherto unknown author in English, early in the process I took the unusual step of proposing a different title altogether: *Fireflies*. Fireflies appear throughout the book as a metaphor for the transcendence of our limited human condition. We start off with an image of the world as a ball of wool and fireflies flying in and out, guiding the knitting needles of the gods. The fireflies seem to be the story-tellers. They take different forms as the multiplicity of characters that cross these pages encounter them: sparks from a fire, a lit cigarette end in the darkness, birds falling from the sky in flames, and of course the stars themselves. They seemed a natural choice for the title.

I was pleased to be vindicated in this decision when I began to correspond with Sagasti by email and he revealed that *Fireflies* – or rather 'Luciérnagas' – was the very name that he had used as a label for the folder on his computer that held his research for the novel. This made for an excellent start to the author-translator relationship, and I was soon seeking his clarification on a number of issues. He would swiftly respond to my questions with generosity and good humour, for which I am grateful.

As an unashamed generalist with a background in philosophy, the book had seemed a natural fit for me. But I soon realised that I had a much more curiously personal connection with the author too. Luis Sagasti was born and still lives in the small city of Bahía Blanca on the Atlantic coast of Argentina, a city known as the gateway to Patagonia. It so happens that half a lifetime ago I made a journey by bicycle from the Pacific coast of Chile along the northern fringes of Patagonia and ending, precisely, in Bahía Blanca. Camping out under the unfamiliar stars of the Southern Hemisphere, I – then an earnest 19-year-old – had written the following in my notebook:

Narrative is that force which urges us to draw a line between any two points, to connect two objects in space with a mental relationship, a story – evident in the continuous mental-visual flitting from point to point, drawing geometric figures, calculating distances, which we constantly engage in. Thus we have conceived of constellations in the skies, so that we can no longer look at the night sky without drawing these lines, we cannot see their illusory nature and the stars simply as points. We are as single stars reclining in silence in the sky and we must be able to imagine ourselves constellated with any other, unbound to the patterns that the perspective of one little planet has forged for us.

To find such a similar idea expressed as one of the central metaphors of *Fireflies* was not only a remarkable coincidence but suggested a deeper affinity with the author. However, too much affinity can be a dangerous thing for a translator. While it is generally more satisfying to translate someone who writes books you like, identifying too closely with your author is one of translation's many perils: in your eagerness to express just how deeply you recognise and share the same feeling or insight, there is a risk of assimilating the author's ideas to your own, of omitting to attend to the small differences of thought and subtleties of expression that are precisely what set it apart as an original. As a translator, you must have the plasticity of thought to go beyond your own knowledge and modes of understanding to let in this newness. It is also important to allow space for ambiguity and multiple interpretations when the original appears to do so.

In the case of this book the challenge lay in the fact that, with little or nothing in the way of plot, characterisation or local detail to grasp on to, it all came down to capturing Sagasti's singular narrative voice. He maintains a very delicate balancing act, the many parts held together by the internal harmonics of the book, by the echoes and repetitions sent back and forth across time and geography. One discordant note, and I feared the whole fragile construction might collapse like a pile of spillikins. It is, at bottom, a performance of the very firefly-inspired storytelling qualities it seeks to describe.

Indeed, in one of the most striking passages in the book – one that reads almost like a manifesto – Sagasti lays down what might be considered a challenge: '...the supreme art of many writers lies in discovering the reverse side of the word even while writing it correctly, as if leaving the door ajar. Perhaps this can be done by placing exactly the right word beside it. As if one were the lock, and the other the key.' How to place exactly the right word, every time, for the many brief, enigmatic sentences that punctuate this text? This proved to be the most demanding aspect of the translation process, and one that required multiple drafts and subtle changes of tone until I was satisfied it captured the book's poignant erudition.

I also had to decide what, amongst the deluge of historical details, were deliberate embellishments and what were accidental errors. Since the very idea of the unreliable narrator and of how myths are formed is so key to the book, I had to judge when to correct a detail, such as the precise type of hat Joseph Beuys always wore, and when to leave it, such as the place in Russia where Yuri Gagarin came back down to Earth. In the latter case, I felt the poetic imagination perfectly justified the change to the reality, while in the former the hat is so much a part of Beuys' persona that to ignore the error would have simply been disconcerting.

There does not seem to be anything particularly 'Argentinian' about the novel, even if a couple of the sections occur in the country. It is in many senses a universal text. Nevertheless, I believe Sagasti's location, on the edge of the great windswept plain of Patagonia, can be felt on every page. I see it as a kind of mirror-image of that seminal work of travel writing, Bruce Chatwin's *In Patagonia*. Chatwin, that great firefly, travelled across Patagonia on foot, constellating the stories of different people linked by that specific geography. Sagasti does the reverse, looking out at the world from his home in Bahía Blanca, on the road to the 'uttermost part of the earth'. It is this remote viewpoint and perspective that allows him to skip so freely between time periods and characters to forge the most unexpected connections between stories from across the globe.

I will finish with an anecdote related by Sagasti that offers a glimpse of where his own narrative urge comes from:

When I was six years old, my grandfather gave me a 12-volume encyclopaedia, chaotic and surprising at the same time, which was called I Know It All. *It was a kind of Google Unplugged, where articles — of which I would only read the captions under the illustrations — went from Troy to silk worms, from the history of the dress to Giuseppe Verdi, and so forth. On turning the page, anything could happen. Perhaps it was this way of accessing knowledge that from the outset influenced me to find hidden links between stories and tales that bear no apparent connection. No doubt this also swayed me to be fascinated by the poetic dimension sometimes carried by pure information.*

As my first book-length fiction translation it was a huge boost to my confidence when *Fireflies* was shortlisted for the UK Translators' Association First Translation Prize 2018, the award established by Daniel Hahn in 2016 that also recognizes the essential and often overlooked work of the editor. In this case my editor was the outstanding Annie McDermott, and looking back at those early drafts it is clear just how much of a collaborative effort this was: I would like to thank her for making it such a rewarding process, despite all the head-scratching it sometimes involved. My deep gratitude, finally, to Carolina and Sam at Charco Press not only for creating this wonderful publishing initiative but for allowing me to be a part of it.

Fionn Petch
Berlin, 2019

CHARCO PRESS

Director/Editor: Carolina Orloff
Director: Samuel McDowell

charcopress.com

Fireflies was published on
90gsm Munken Premium Cream paper.

The text was designed using
Bembo 11 and ITC Galliard Pro.

Printed in September 2019 by TJ International.
Padstow, Cornwall PL28 8RW using responsibly sourced
paper and environmentally-friendly adhesive.